SANTOSH JOSHI

MANY LIVES ONE SOUL

Published in India by :
EMBASSY BOOK DISTRIBUTORS,
120, Great Western Building,
Maharashtra Chamber of Commerce Lane,
Kala Ghoda, Fort,
Mumbai- 400 023.
Tel : (+91-22) 2281 9546 / 32967415
Email :info@embassybooks.in
www.embassybooks.in

Illustrations by Santosh Joshi

ISBN: 978-93-85492-15-0

Disclaimer: Examples given in the book are inspired by real life stories. We have changed some names and actual details to maintain and respect the privacy of the concerned persons.

Printed in India by Repro India Ltd.

To all the divine souls,
on this journey
Seeking answers and
looking for a key,
I dedicate this book,
to help them see
Beyond the ordinary,
to set themselves free...

TABLE OF CONTENTS

ACKNOWLEDGEMENTS

I feel gratified that my first book KEYS has impacted many lives and given a direction to the readers who wish to live a happy and regret-free life. The divine grace of my guru – *Swami Nityananda of Ganeshpuri*, and the love and support from my readers, has made KEYS the best-seller in a span of less than two years.

I am blessed to have my wife and soul-mate Aruna always by my side. It is amazing to walk the path holding each other's hands towards a common purpose. All I can say is that this book would not have been possible without your support. You are my friend on whom I can depend, a philosopher who helps me see the truth, and a guide who shows me the way when I am lost. Thanks for believing in me and helping me follow my heart and passion.

I am eternally grateful to my parents for their love and support. No words of gratitude will suffice for all the sacrifices they made to provide the best to their children. Sincere thanks to my parents-in-law for always being understanding and showing confidence in my abilities.

This book became a reality only because Sohin Lakhani, CEO of Embassy books, showed keen interest and published it.

Sohin, I am ever grateful to you for being such an important part of my journey. It's been pleasure working together and happy to have found a new friend in you.

My heartfelt thanks to Meirah Bhastekar for taking time out of her busy schedule and editing this book. Thanks to Madhu Sahoo, Sakshi Issar, Bhavin Purohit for their valuable contribution. Thanks to Megha Meshram for assisting me in all my Past life regression workshops and sessions.

Many thanks to Sonal Churi for designing such a fabulous cover for my book.

The seed of PLR therapy was sown by Dr. Lakshmi and Dr. Newton Kondaveti. It was under their able guidance that I got my first PLR experience and learnt the therapy. My heartfelt thanks to both of them.

There are a few souls whose massive support has made easy for Aruna and I to walk on the chosen path. Our domestic help Shabana khan and our cook Kiran Devrukhkar, who are an important part of our family. Sunil Choudhary, who is just a call away and always ready to help. Truly grateful to them for their endless support. I am blessed to have such divine souls in my life.

Special thanks to Anju Musafir, Pascal Chazot, Ashutosh Chicholikar, Riny Sengupta, Kanika Bahl, Dipti Gandhi for sharing their story and experiences in this book.

There are a few people who were not directly involved with the book, but their contribution to my life's journey is worth a mention. I take this opportunity to thank my sister Manisha and brother-in-law Kishor, Arati - Aniruddha, Shweta - Santa, Vaishali - Rakesh, Priti - Amit, Shivratan Singrodia, Suma

Varughese, Subhank Rajguru, Nitin Deshmukh and Sanjay Beswal.

A special thanks to all my batch-mates of 1990 batch of MITS, for their encouragement, active support and being friends for life.

I have developed a modality called SKY Healing and I recently made SKY teachers to spread this amazing technique. I am highly grateful to all the SKY teachers for believing in me and my teachings and taking the initiative to help me reach SKY to more and more people.

Last but not the least, a big thanks to all my workshop participants and those who have undergone personal sessions with me, for your trust and love. You have been a great inspiration for this book.

KEYS
WHO AM I...?
FUNDAMENTAL QUESTIONS
FIRST ANSWER THIS QUESTION...
WHERE WERE YOU LAST NIGHT... ?

PREFACE

It was 16th June, 1999.

Monsoon had begun in India. The Rain God seemed to be particularly pleased with Mumbai, while the rest of the country was still parched. On that day, it had been pouring incessantly since the early morning. Heavy rains created water logging everywhere leading to worst ever traffic jams. It was 3pm and I was sitting in a cab heading back home from work. I looked out of the window. The sky had turned tar-black, as the sun buried itself under the ferocious dark clouds. The street lamps went on before time but were barely able to sweep away the darkness.

It seemed as if the dark clouds of my thoughts were projected in the sky, breaking into huge droplets of water and drenching the entire city in melancholy. The hammering noise of the droplets banging on the roof of the cab irritated me to the core. I was experiencing an all time emotional low. Everyone on the street seemed to be eager to reach home, except me. Half-way there, I changed my mind and instructed the cab driver to take a detour towards the sea-facing promenade which was about two kilometers from my workplace.

When I got there, I sat on a bench, and despite the rains soaking me through, lost myself in my thoughts. There was a deep hollow within me, filled with frustration and anger – at myself and everybody around me. My heart was bleeding, and there was a sharp pain in my chest.

The last few years flashed in front of my eyes. As a senior manager in a reputed corporate house, I had invested blood, sweat and tears every day into my work, with utmost honesty and dedication. A colleague, who was also my best buddy, framed me, and I became a victim of his ambition and ego. Like a fool I had been completely unaware of things brewing behind my back. I certainly did not deserve this.

Earlier that day, I had resigned. More than the feeling of victimhood, it was the deceit of a close friend that defeated me. I failed to understand, how someone I trusted so much, could do something so terrible. I was drowning in a plethora of negative emotions and a tsunami of questions – why did this happen to me? what wrongs had I done to deserve this?, transported me into a miserable zone.

In order to find answers to these questions, over the next few months, I visited several astrologers, numerologists and palmists. None gave me an answer that satisfied me.

Life is like a river, they say. It does not leave you at one place to rot. It drags you ahead with its flow to a new destination. This happened with me as well. After a year of distress, I found my dream job, which evened out everything in my life. Because I had been pushed out of my comfort zone, I had found a better career opportunity; my life changed for the better and there was no looking back.

It was then that I realized that everything that happens in our life does happen for a reason, a greater purpose and our highest good.

The search that had begun that rainy evening by the sea ended when I discovered Past Life Regression (PLR). Based on the theory of reincarnation and karma, PLR is a tool to understand and interpret the underlying subtle patterns of life.

In a simple and convincing manner, it untied the knots of one of the most complicated situations of my life, and gave my existence a higher meaning by revealing my life's purpose to me.

I still get goose bumps when I remember the metaphysical experience I had during a PLR session. In a crystal-clear vision, I could see my life's purpose, which was 'to walk on the path of healing, and help people come out of their miseries and traumas'. It was also revealed to me why my wife and I do not have children. I found that we have a common purpose in this life, and we are together to fulfil it – we are here to work for a cause and will be guided, protected and provided all through. Such profound experiences are very difficult to describe within the confines of words, though. I was so convinced with this experience that I quit my lucrative career in the corporate world to follow this purpose.

One thing I knew for sure, every incident in my life, big or small, relevant or irrelevant; and every person I meet has a significant role to play in defining my life. Some of them support me whole-heartedly, some throw immeasurable challenges on the way but each one eventually paves a way towards my purpose.

Underlying patterns of life

If we look at one lifetime, each experience, however small it may be, contributes to the shaping of life as a whole. All these experiences put together ultimately form a beautiful pattern. Sometimes there are also subtle patterns that seem illogical, and defy our normal perceptions but they may have a deeper meaning that we are not able to decode.

If we are able to perceive these underlying patterns of life, we will be able to see the world in a different way, with more clarity and better understanding. This can help us achieve greater success and happiness, creating a masterpiece on the canvas of life.

The award-winning American novelist and journalist Chuck Palahniuk famously said, "What we call chaos is just patterns we haven't recognized. What we call random is just patterns we can't decipher."

This book is about these varied underlying patterns of our life and how they affect and shape it.

Why should one believe in life after death and the theory of reincarnation?

While there may not be a scientific explanation to this phenomenon, Eastern philosophies have always supported the theories of reincarnation and karma, and Eastern scriptures are full of examples and explanations of them.

I encourage you to think about this – if this current life each of us is leading is the only life we have ever and will ever live, what would the explanation be for the vast disparity in the world. Why are some people born rich and some poor? Why are some people born with physical disabilities? Why do certain people have phobias? It would be difficult to believe that life is good if there was nothing beyond the grave to compensate for problems like inequality and unfairness.

From the ancient Eastern cultures to modern-day Western thinkers, it is widely believed that the soul survives death, and extensive research has been done in the West to prove this. The phenomenon of the soul living after death has been mentioned in religious scriptures that predate science, which is just a few hundred years old.

A lot of documentation has been done on people, especially children, who remember their past lives. Such instances have also been validated. Edgar Cayce, Dr. Michael Newton, Dr. Brien Weiss and Dr. Ian Stevenson are a few pioneers in this field.

In fact, belief in the theory of reincarnation provides one with personal security, optimism and spiritual betterment. It helps in dealing with the challenges of the present life with more confidence, courage and positivity, offering hope for a better life ahead. It also provides answers to questions that have no logical explanation.

People who attend my workshops or personal sessions have a lot of questions, which we all think about on a day-to-day basis. I have tried to answer most of these questions through this book. It is amazing how PLR not only helps one understand 'why things happen the way they do' but also effectively heals many issues.

I have used real-life examples throughout this book. Although at some places, names and context of the people involved have been changed to protect their identity, as such experiences are very personal.

I am sure, anybody who has questions such as, 'Why me?' can find logical and convincing answers through this book, gaining a greater understanding of life.

Life is a celebration

While I was in the process of writing this book, a friend asked me, "Are you going to have your signature cartoons in this book as well, like you had in KEYS?"

"Of course, yes," I said.

"But I thought this book deals with some serious questions and deeper aspects of life."

"Absolutely, it does."

He looked puzzled by my reply.

Very often we feel that life is a serious business. And for sure, there are hardships, challenges, unnerving situations that may tear us apart. But the fact is that we cannot exit these challenging situations without passing through them. If this is inevitable, then why not soldier through trying situations with a smile?

A dash of humour lessens the intensity of any situation, helping us deal with it in a better way. Based on this philosophy, I have added cartoons in each chapter to make the book an easy and light read. I believe life is all about celebration, however challenging it may be at times. Challenges come in our life only to make us better and they should not prevent us from having fun. We just need to shift our point of view.

How to read this book?

Since each chapter delves deep into a question, you can choose a chapter or question at random, that which resonates with you. However, I suggest reading it in the sequence in which it has been written, as I have also weaved in the theories of evolution and karmas through each chapter. Every chapter ends with an Essence, which can be used as a quick reference, and the blank space provided - 'Reflections', is for you to record your thoughts and observations. If you read the chapters of this book as a parallel to your own life, I am sure you will find answers to the questions that are on your mind. There is also an exercise in the end which will help you evaluate your progress on the journey of evolution.

May you find the answers you are looking for...

Santosh Joshi
September, 2015

1

WHY ME?

RESUME
INTERVIEW
HE HAS A MAGNETIC PERSONALITY...
HE ATTRACTS DISASTERS...

1

For the challenges in life, big or small
There's a lesson to be learnt, by one and all
"Why me?" if we ask at every fall
We may miss the bell of destiny's call

The legendary tennis player with three Grand Slam titles to his credit, Arthur Ashe was diagnosed with AIDS, due to infected blood transfusion, during a heart surgery in 1983.

He received letters from grief-stricken fans from the world over. One of them wrote: "Why did God select you for such a bad disease?"

To this Arthur Ashe replied, "The world over, 50,000,000 children start playing tennis, 5,000,000 learn to play tennis, 500,000 learn professional tennis, 50,000 come to the circuit, 5000 reach the Grand

Slam, 50 reach the Wimbledon, four to semi-finals, two to finals. When I was the one holding the cup, I never asked God, "Why me?" And today in pain, I should not be asking God, "Why me?"

Don't we blame God or destiny for all the unpleasant things that happen in our lives?

If a colleague gets a promotion and we don't, we get depressed.

If we have one bad relationship in our life, we sulk.

If we face health issues, we curse God.

If we lose someone close to us, our life becomes a disaster.

If somebody cheats us, our life is ruined.

When life throws too many challenges at us we become dejected, and the perennial thought crosses our mind – "Why me?"

Julie worked with a corporate house, as a secretary to the managing director and earned a decent pay. She lived in Mumbai with her husband and daughter and was a happy camper, until the day her husband lost his job. It was a big blow, for now she had to wear more than one hat. The responsibility of maintaining the family's standard of living in a city like Mumbai now lay on her shoulders.

As the family was trying to come to terms with the situation, Julie's boss called her into his office one morning and asked her to resign. She was a victim of office politics and now her boss wanted to replace her. Julie had no choice but to do as he asked, even though she had worked in the firm for 18 long years. Depressed, Julie often complained to God and asked, "Why me?". Unable to cope with her situation, as she was serving out her notice period, she fainted in the office.

Her blood pressure shot up and she had to be admitted to a hospital. After the initial treatment, she came back to consciousness. Doctors advised her to be in the hospital for a few days.

Next morning, the doctor came for a visit to her room and they began talking. "What is troubling you, Julie?" the doctor asked.

She told him her story. He listened and said, with a smile, "We have an urgent need for an office assistant. Would you mind joining us?"

The doctor offered her double the salary she had been earning at her previous job. It was more than she could have ever asked for. When her boss had asked her to leave, Julie had assumed that her life was doomed. And just few days later, she got a much better job and the answer to her question, "why me?".

We get perturbed by the challenges that we face, but if we look at all the situations in retrospect, we can understand why things happened the way they did. These situations teach us an important lesson — let go and move on. The art lies in how soon we stop looking at the closed door and walk towards new doors that open up to new horizons.

The problem arises when we stay victims in a challenging situation. Sometimes we become so complacent that we unknowingly refuse to let go of what we are holding on to. We thrive on the feeling of victimhood, unable to recognize the gifts showered upon us by life.

An acquaintance of mine had a terrible marriage, and suffered for almost a decade. She lived with her in-laws in a joint family and she was ill-treated by them, which caused her great trauma. After about 10 years, she moved out of the house with her husband and lived independently. However, even today whenever we meet, she talks only about that decade of distress.

She said to me once, "I want to try past life regression. I am curious to find out how my in-laws were related to me in my past birth. They made my life miserable."

"Sure we can. But what is the problem now? You are the master of your own life. I feel it is high time you let go of the past", I replied.

"You don't understand, Santosh. It is easier said than done. They have spoiled ten beautiful years of my life. How can I let go?" she said, in an irritated tone.

She was right. I really failed to understand her, why she was unable to let go. Why was she spoiling her entire life by not letting go? She had completely ensconced herself in the comfort zone of victimhood. Even when I tried to convince her to let go, she totally ignored. She was thriving on the sympathy gained from people around her.

Aren't we, most often responsible for situations in our life? Still, we blame God for our anguish.

And isn't there always a lesson to be learnt from every situation in life?

The deeper secrets

My 55-year-old banker friend suffered a stroke two years back. He was hospitalized for a couple of weeks and was advised three months of complete bed rest. The entire family was overwhelmed. The physical and mental stress and the never ending hospital bills did leave them in despair; but only for a short time.

What was remarkable was how after the initial shock, he and his family accepted the situation in a very positive way. When I visited him after three weeks of being in the hospital, he was the same happy person he has always been, cracking jokes and laughing heartily. I could hardly believe that he had suffered a massive stroke just a few weeks back.

"How did it happen?" I asked him, with concern.

"Hey, don't worry, it was just a small correction that took place in my life," he replied cheerfully. Then with an impish smile and a twinkle in his eyes he added, "You know the biggest positive outcome of my stroke? Now I no longer have to prove to my wife that I have a heart."

"And as a result of this stroke, all his girlfriends have left his heart," his wife added teasingly, and we all had a laugh.

But on a serious note, his words "correction in life" appealed to me. His lifestyle had a complete makeover after this incident. He switched to a healthier and gratifying life.

Often, we just ignore our body, which is a vehicle meant to take us through the fascinating journey of life. The universe has its own way of making corrections, if we are off-track.

Ever since I have experienced PLR and helped others undergo it, I have realized that every situation or event in our life has a deeper meaning. Our perception of a circumstance being good or bad is only the result of logical reasoning and deep conditioning. The events in my life that I thought were bad, led to something very beautiful eventually. Now I have come to believe that everything in this universe works perfectly. We just need to change our perspective and look at the larger picture. The attitude does matter.

You may have heard stories of the famous Mughal emperor Akbar and his wise minister Birbal. Akbar took his minister wherever he went. Once while hunting in a forest, Akbar cut his toe. His was in deep pain. On seeing the bleeding toe, his wise minister commented, "Everything happens for a greater good." Akbar was furious at this statement and ordered his men to put Birbal behind bars. Then he asked Birbal, "What do you have to say now?" He repeated, "Everything happens for a greater good." Thinking that Birbal has lost his mind, Akbar left him there and went back to the forest. After sunset, he lost his way in the dark and was left alone. While walking, he was caught by some tribes-men who decided to offer him as sacrifice to their goddess. Just as the emperor was readied to be beheaded, a person from the crowd noticed that his toe was bleeding. There was a lot of deliberation and eventually, Akbar was set free, as offering a person with an injured toe was considered inauspicious.

On reaching back, Akbar apologized to Birbal and freed him from the prison.

Akbar said, "You were imprisoned without committing a serious mistake. How was that good for you?"

To which Birbal politely replied, "Your highness, if I was with you, they would have offered me as sacrifice. I am safe only because you put me in jail."

Even if we agree that 'whatever happens in our life is for our highest good', other significant questions still remain unanswered:

Why there are problems in life?

Why there is disparity in the world?

Why don't some relationships work?

Why do bad things happen to good people?

We mull over these and several other such questions frequently without getting anywhere.

Occasionally, when we start thinking about life and its deeper meaning, we also come across the 'fundamental questions about our existence and purpose'. This is the time we start questioning life itself. I was very young when I closely witnessed the death of a relative. Having just stepped into the corporate environment, I was living in the world of cut-throat competition, stress and one-upmanship. I was very ambitious and wanted to reach the top. But this particular incident stirred something deep within me. It made me reflect on my life. The sudden realization that even I have to leave this world one day, surfaced in my mind. I was disturbed by these thoughts. The hurricane of questions shook me to my core.

Where do I come from?

Where do I go?

Have I lived before?

What happens after death?

What is the purpose of my life?

And most importantly,

Who am I?

The search for the answers to these questions, led me to the deeper truths of life. And life after life.

— ESSENCE —

EVERYTHING IN THIS UNIVERSE WORKS PERFECTLY...

WE JUST NEED TO CHANGE OUR PERSPECTIVE, AND LOOK AT THE LARGER PICTURE...

Reflections

2

WHY DO I HAVE PROBLEMS IN LIFE?

REMEMBER, EACH PROBLEM IS GIVING YOU A LESSON FOR YOUR GROWTH...

2

All things bright & beautiful,
all creatures great & small

It's part of our journey,
we've been through them all.

Problems are only to learn from
and evolve through the process

They're just positive roadblocks,
to make us stand tall.

What if I say, problems are nothing but positive roadblocks for self-development?

Some of you may think I am crazy, close the book and walk away from it. Now, if I add that we are the ones who plan our challenges or problems in our life, you may think I don't know what I am talking about. "Why would any sane person create challenges or problems in their life?"

I request you to try this simple exercise, before we actually dig deeper.

Put your favourite relaxing music, or try my relaxation meditation CD. Take a few deep breaths and start to relax. Focus on your breath. Observe your breath as it goes deep inside your belly and comes out. Slowly let your eyes close. As you become more and more relaxed, your awareness expands. You slowly cut off from the noise around you. What you can hear now is only the sound of your breath.

As you are with yourself now, take a tour down memory lane. Bring to your conscious awareness, a period of your life when you faced maximum challenges. Re-experience all the problems one by one.

Experience the feelings you went through at that time. Were you sad, or depressed, angry or guilty, filled with regret or helplessness? Concentrate on the negative feelings you went through during that time.

Focus on these feelings. Which part of your body are these feelings coming from? Take your attention to that part of the body. Give that feeling a colour and a shape.

Treat this part of the body as a separate entity. Talk to this entity. What are these negative feelings telling you? Listen carefully to what they have to say. There is a lesson to be learnt from the challenges you faced and from the feelings attached to these challenges.

Once you have learnt the lesson they are trying to teach you, change this colour and shape to a positive one. Experience that positive colour filling your entire body.

Slowly come back to the present situation. Open your eyes and take a few minutes to ponder on what you experienced before you go ahead to read further.

I recently met Ashutosh Chincholikar, an old friend from engineering college, after almost 22 years. His wife Nayani is a doctor. When their first daughter, Shivani was born, they both were very happy and relished every moment of parenthood. All was well, until one day Nayani noticed some twitching on the baby's face, arms and limbs. Being a doctor, she suspected that something was not right. The baby was only 40 days old then. Thorough investigations revealed that the baby was suffering from Lennox-Gastaut-Syndrome (LGS), also known as Lennox syndrome. This meant that the child would have physical and intellectual disabilities and as the disease progresses, she would get frequent seizures. The family was heartbroken. But very soon, they accepted this challenge, and decided to raise their daughter in the best possible way.

Today Shivani is almost 20. When I met them, I was literally in tears, amazed at the greatness of my friend and his family. This girl was on a wheelchair, physically inactive, but was groomed like a princess – very well-dressed with neatly combed hair. The smile on her face was contagious. Her whole being radiated happiness and contentment because of all the unconditional love showered upon her by my friend, his wife and family.

I was deeply touched by what I saw. Having your child diagnosed with such a syndrome presents any parent with a huge challenge. And my friend and his family had accepted the challenge with utmost grace. Not even once during our conversation did he complain or show his displeasure about this situation.

On the contrary, he said, "This is a challenge in our life we have to go through. What our child demands from us is only our love and attention, which we are giving. Children suffering from LGS often suffer a lot, but we are so fortunate to have a child who is responsive and jovial."

"But let me tell you, Santosh" he added modestly, "this particular situation in our life has taught us great lessons that no school in this world could ever have – humility, acceptance and unconditional love. We now firmly believe that a superpower exists. We both are doing very well in our respective careers, but this situation in our life keeps us completely grounded."

I was speechless.

Whenever we face any challenge in life, we always have a choice – we can either whine about the problems and be miserable, or accept them as a learning curve, do the best we can and emerge a winner.

Adverse situations hold the most invaluable lessons of life. In fact, I would rate them as the real parameters of growth. If we are able to successfully navigate the challenges life throws at us, we automatically progress to the next level.

The theory of reincarnation illustrates this best. Since I came across these theories, my perspective towards life has changed completely.

Concept of reincarnation

As humans, we are on the earth plane, which is the most basic level of existence. Along with the earth plane, there are seven other planes on a subtle level. These planes cannot be perceived by our sense organs but do exist in the same place. Primarily, earth is considered as a school and we are the students. As souls, we house ourselves in a physical body, so that we can learn the lessons meant for our own evolutionary progress. As souls, we are part of a bigger source or super energy. At the time of birth, we come to the earth plane, live our lives, develop ourselves through our experiences here and go back at the time of our death to the subtle planes. The time we spend in the subtle planes is also called the Life Between Life (LBL) state. In this state, we meet our masters and guiding angels with whom we review the life we have just lived and plan the next one. This is also the resting period for the soul.

In this process, we learn and advance life after life, until the time we are ready to go back and mix with the infinite source of which we are a part.

So why do we face problems in our lives? There is a theory to it. Before we take birth in a physical body, we design our life on earth at soul level with the help of our masters. We choose the parents we are going to be born to, the place where we will be born, the challenges, the situation or circumstances in our life, and the people who are going to be associated with us.

We also decide the time of our exit from the earth plane. The challenges or problems we plan for our life help us grow and evolve. They take us closer to our own real self. This is why I maintain that problems are nothing but positive roadblocks to self-development.

Though the situations and associations in our life are pre-decided, we have been given the free will, and the choice – through our intellect – to choose how to react to challenges. This paves the way to our destiny and our future. When we overcome these challenges, we transcend them and evolve by learning an important lesson every time.

This process goes on for many lifetimes. It is said that on an average we spend about 600 to 700 lifetimes as humans, for complete spiritual evolution, after which we attain *enlightenment* or *nirvana* and go back to the source from which we came. After this process is complete, we have a choice to come back on the earth plane but with a responsibility of guiding the masses to evolve and grow.

This process is created in a way that we remember all of this until the age of three or four, after which an iron curtain is drawn between us and the subtle world. As we grow older, our memory of the LBL state starts fading slowly. We get carried away by the things around us and get trapped in belief systems, conditioning and dogmas formed by us and others, which disconnect us from our own true self.

In my workshops on past life regression, I am often confronted with one recurring question, which I am sure you have thought about too - "If we, as souls, decide everything in our life before coming on this earth, then why is it said that we create our own destiny?"

As I have explained in my book KEYS, the future is nothing but a matrix of possibilities. It is in a fluid state. Our reaction or response to every situation in our life leads us to the next step.

In case of my friend Ashutosh, he had a choice to either be dejected by the situation and curse God, or accept and learn the lessons that his child could teach him. The second choice hastens our soul's growth. Moreover, these challenges keep coming in our lives until we learn the lessons we are meant to.

If we understand the process of evolution, we will never see challenges as problems, but as opportunities to learn from and grow. Such challenging situations often bring out our highest potential and take us closer to the purpose of life.

I recently read a soul-stirring story of 24-year-old Arunima Sinha from Lucknow. In May 2011, Arunima was travelling to Delhi for a job interview, when she was thrown off a moving train by thugs for refusing to hand over the gold necklace she was wearing. She fell on the tracks and another train went over her left leg. She lay on the tracks, bleeding and screaming in pain. She could see that her left leg was almost detached from her body and rodents were feeding on her flesh and blood, but she was unable to move. After hours in this situation, she was rescued and taken to the nearby district hospital. The hospital was out of oxygen cylinders, anaesthesia and blood. Doctors were hesitant to treat her under such conditions. Her leg had to be amputated as gangrene had started to set in. With great courage, she told the doctors that they must operate on her without anaesthesia. Later when her family arrived, she was shifted to AIIMS in Delhi.

While she was battling for her life in the hospital, she became a media sensation. Stories speculated that she had tried to commit suicide, and Arunima was not in a state to defend herself and her family against this onslaught. Lying on the hospital bed, she made a decision - "'Today is your day. Bark whatever you want. But someday I will prove, without a doubt, the truth of what happened to me.' My left leg is amputated. A rod has been inserted in my right leg, from the knee to the ankle, to hold the shattered bones together. What is the most impossible goal I can set for myself right now? I will climb Mount Everest".

Life was throwing challenges at her at every step, testing her resolve, but Arunima chose to face them, "Every girl cannot climb Everest to prove herself right. But for me it was never a choice. The public imagination had reduced me to either a victim or an attempted suicide case. This was the only way I could reclaim my voice. When I tried to discuss my plan with anyone, I was either laughed off or told that the trauma had affected my mental health adversely."

Fighting all odds and with a prosthetic limb, she went to meet Bachendri Pal, the first Indian woman to climb Everest. Pal told her, "Arunima, in this condition you made such a huge decision. Know that you have already conquered your inner Everest. Now you need to climb the mountain, only to show the world what you are made of."

After being rigorously trained by Pal and with help from a sponsorship by Tata Steel, Arunima set out to achieve her goal. Her challenges had only just begun. Her prosthetic limb posed some unique problems – her ankle and heel would constantly swivel as she tried to climb, causing her to lose her grip often.

Her right leg was held together by a steel rod, so any pressure on it sent up spasms of acute pain. Her Sherpa almost refused to accompany her, convinced that Arunima was on a suicide mission.

Finally as she reached Camp Four from where the summit was 3500 feet, her Sherpa informed her that her oxygen supply was critically low and advised her to go back. She said to herself, "If I don't climb Everest now, my life will not have been worth saving." With renewed zest and tenacity Arunima climbed up to the peak, with help from an oxygen cylinder she found discarded by someone on the way. They say that God favours the brave. And Arunima became the world's first female amputee to climb Mount Everest. In 2013, she was awarded Padma Shri, the fourth highest civilian award in India.

When Arunima faced the most adverse and enduring challenges at every step in her life, she always had a choice. She could have easily given up and led a victimized life thriving on the sympathies of people around her. But she chose to evolve through this ordeal, by displaying immense fortitude, and set an example for generations to come.

— ESSENCE —

ADVERSE SITUATIONS HOLD THE MOST INVALUABLE LESSONS OF LIFE.

IF WE ARE ABLE TO TRANSCEND THESE, WE AUTOMATICALLY CLIMB THE SPIRITUAL LADDER TO THE NEXT LEVEL...

Reflections

3

WHY DON'T MY RELATIONSHIPS WORK?

HONEY, YOU LOOK FAB...!!
AND THE REST IS HISTORY...

3

We are divine souls,
on journey of evolution
Helping each other grow,
whatever the relation
Filled with love sometime,
sometimes challenges
But all the time moving to
reach the destination

Karen, who currently works in Dubai, is an only child and her family lives in Canada. She had a troubled relationship with her father, since childhood. A couple of years ago, her dad was diagnosed with cancer and his health started to deteriorate slowly. Whenever he spoke to Karen over phone, the conversation would be very precise and abrupt. She had pent up every issue that she had ever faced with her father, from when she was a child, that she was now completely closed off from him. He would plead with her to come and visit him at least once. But Karen always made an excuse about her work, and refused every time. When she got time off from work, she chose to go to New Zealand with her boyfriend, and when she was there, Karen got the news of her father's death.

She was completely devastated, and angry with herself for never having visited him, even when he had pleaded with her to. This led to her feeling very guilty, because the knowledge that she would never see her father again played on her mind all the time. She had lost her chance to make peace with him. Strangely, though, after he passed away, she only remembered all the good times she had spent with her father.

Why do we have sour relationships with some people - even our parents and dear ones? Why do we hate certain people at first sight? Why do good relationships sometimes end in an unpleasant way? Why is it that the person we dearly love hates us? Why do certain people move away from us, even after a long association? Why don't we share the same vibes with people, who were our best friends earlier?

Or on the other hand, why do some people fall in love at first sight? Why do certain people suddenly come in our lives and stay forever? Why it is that strangers sometimes come forward to help and support us? Why do we feel that magnetic pull in some relationships?

I had once heard an old gentleman say, "We don't need to find reasons for the good things happening in life; but we must make an effort to get to the root of bad things. There are a lot of lessons hidden there."

At some point in life, each one of us asks at least one of the above questions. People let years go by, without knowing why things are going wrong, while blaming the entire world for their problems. Some go through their share of issues, completely oblivious of the silver lining that exists. Although it is often said that everything happens for a reason, life can be extremely frustrating for those who don't understand this truth.

I had a few close friends who meant the world to me but they drifted away without any valid reason. Like everyone else, I also wondered why and only later did I understand that each person we come across in life has a reason for their association with us. Past life regression helps us accept that reason and evolve further. It could be a lesson to be learnt or simply some past life karma that needs to be released. Once that is done, that person slowly moves away from our lives.

Karmic connections

Thirty-three-year-old Mansi visited me in a very disturbed state of mind, because of her bitter divorce. She truly loved her husband and had sacrificed a lot to be with him, but five years into the marriage, he had fallen in love with someone else. Even though they had a three-year-old daughter together, Mansi's husband abandoned her. She was completely depressed and wanted to know why this had happened to her. We decided to do a regression session, in order to find her answers.

Mansi quickly went into a trance, in which she was drawn into the memory of a life she had lived about 200 years back. She had been a powerful zamindar (landowner) in North India. This zamindar was wealthy, and had several wives, one of whom he treated very badly and subjected to much trauma and sorrow. That wife was Mansi's husband in this life.

In the life-between-life state, Mansi understood that the karmas between them had to be settled in this lifetime and once she did, her outlook towards life changed. She accepted all the issues and challenges she was facing.

In another case, Shilpa complained to me about being ill-treated by her mother-in-law. During regression, she saw that her mother-in-law had been her sister in a previous lifetime and in that lifetime, Shilpa had made her sister's life miserable. So in this life, that sister chose to be her mother-in-law to settle the karmas. After undergoing the therapy, Shilpa could empathize with her mother-in-law but asked me a very valid question - "Well, I may change my perspective of looking at my mother-in-law, but what about her? She will not change."

I said to her, "You are right, Shilpa. Remember that you are an independent soul on your own journey and are responsible only for yourself. Moreover, if you resolve the issue at your end, it will lose its hold on you. When you stop reacting, it will positively impact your mother-in-law as well."

Shilpa was satisfied with my answer and later, I came to know that from her experience with PLR, Shilpa was able to take her relationship with her mother-in-law to a different level. The common belief that all mother-in-law and daughter-in-law relationships are strained can be done away with, as the basis of all our relationships are karmas. I have come across many daughters-in-law who share a very close bond with their mothers-in-law, sometimes one closer than with their own mothers.

This is how karma works. It is a natural process and an infallible law that governs our lives, whether we are conscious about it or not. It may take years, even lifetimes, to fructify but it eventually catches up. Relationships are a significant part of our existence. They are the core essence of our being. The credit or debit in our karma account is a result of our relationships. Our karmas are influenced by our thoughts, words and actions.

We are all connected at the soul level. In fact, the people we are related to come from the same soul group, which is a group of infinite beings of consciousness, who help each other learn life's lessons. Many have been with us in previous incarnations and have spent the majority of time with us in the ethereal realms. While we're on the 'other side', we make agreements with our soul group's members to meet at some juncture in our earth-bound lives. When we meet someone for the first time and develop an instant rapport as if we have known them forever, it is a sign that they are from our soul group. Souls from the same soul group not only offer lessons but also help us take our relationships at a higher level. The common thread binding every relationship is love, which is the purest form of energy pervading universally. In helping our soul mates grow and evolve, we also settle our karmas with them.

In Mansi's case, had she refused to accept that her husband cheated on her, and if she had not forgiven him, she would have ended up creating more karmas through her thoughts and actions, and then face similar situations in the future. But because of the higher understanding she gained during the process of regression, she could let go of the bitter feelings, forgive him and move on in life.

Sometimes, it becomes difficult to relate to a person with whom we had a very close association in the past; for example, someone may have been our best buddy in school but he or she seems so distant when we meet after 20-25 years. As explained earlier, we need to understand that we are souls at different levels of evolution, and even during one lifetime we keep going back and forth between those different levels. Hence we meet the people, who are on the same plane as us, and we disconnect from those who are not, but the dynamics keep changing and we may cross paths again, depending on our karmic debts with that person.

Raziya who is now 29, was in a relationship with David for almost 12 years. Their different religions created a block for their relationship to flourish. Interfaith weddings are still not readily accepted in some parts of India. They were committed to one another and wanted to spend the rest of their lives together. After about 12 years of the relationship, when David's mother realized that she could not separate them, she attempted suicide. Being the only son, David was left with no choice than to end his relationship with Raziya and get engaged to a girl of his mother's choice. Raziya was totally heart-broken by this act and went into severe depression. She couldn't believe that David could do this.

Belonging to a faith that does not subscribe to the theory of reincarnation, Raziya was reluctant to experience a past life regression session. However, more than actually visiting a past life memory, it was important for Raziya to accept the situation and move on; because the more she was stuck the more prone she was to take a drastic step.

However, her trust in me made her decision easy. I decided to take her through a session of 'Meeting your Master', a beautiful exercise in which, in the state of trance, we come face to face with our master or guiding angel who has been guiding us through all our lifetimes. Raziya was shocked at the message she received during the session – she saw that she and David have been coming together in previous lifetimes as well, in different relationships. Before coming to this lifetime, they had decided to face this situation as a challenge to learn 'detachment'. If they could successfully go through this, it would take their relationship to the next level. Raziya also learnt that they will come together again in the next lifetime.

This message gave some solace to Raziya's distressed soul. Slowly she came to terms with reality and moved on in life, though she decided not to marry.

That love-hate relationship may start in the womb

One morning, 18-year-old Karishma walked into my office. A tall, fair girl with long hair, she was my youngest client ever and carried herself in a dignified manner that suggested she was in control of her life.

Though she displayed a cool demeanour, I could tell that there was a barrage of emotions in her just waiting to explode. Karishma was in complete denial of her emotional turbulence but I could easily sense her rising anxiety levels and her deep inner conflict. She was afraid to be vulnerable, and, at the same time, wanted a solution for her problem.

"So, tell me, Karishma, what brings you here?"

"Actually, I have some issues with my mom," she said, looking a little disturbed.

"Feel free to discuss it with me. We can surely find a solution."

"I hate my mom but don't know why. She is quite loving and caring, but somehow I don't like her. This has been bothering me for the longest time. At times, I am very rude to her and later I feel guilty about my behaviour," Karishma confessed, in tears.

I let her cry for a while and said, "I am here to help you, Karishma. Don't worry. We shall try and find out the reason for this."

"But why should I hate my own mother? The issues between two of us are increasing day by day. It's impossible for us to stay under one roof."

As we spoke about it more, it was clear that there was no apparent reason for her hatred. The answer was beyond the obvious. I decided to do a present-life regression session with her to access the memories forgotten by the conscious mind; this was the only way to get to the root cause of the issue Karishma was facing. She agreed, and we began the session.

There was no memory till the age of one from the present, which could establish the connection with the issue. Though she could recollect a lot of unpleasant moments shared with her mother.

When I guided her to the womb state, I was amazed at what came up. She went to a point where she experienced herself being in the mother's womb as a three-month-old foetus. She could feel that her mother was not happy with the conception. Karishma started facing rejection from there on – "I am unwanted. My mother wants to kill me."

Karishma's body language changed while she was in deep trance in my office. She was scared. Her mother had made up her mind to abort the baby. It was an early pregnancy and her parents were not ready. However, the doctor was not supportive of her decision and warned her of the risk involved in doing so. After counselling with the doctor and other family members, her mother agreed to go ahead with the pregnancy. Once she accepted this, she was happy. Soon, she gave birth to a beautiful baby and lovingly named her Karishma, which meant a miracle.

All was well in the end, but the feeling of rejection from her own mother, the insecurity and the fear of being killed was so deeply embedded in Karishma when she was a foetus that it stayed with her even today.

During that session, I made Karishma communicate with her mother. (In the level of trance you can connect to any soul through your thoughts.) This exercise cleared a lot of misunderstandings, as her mother told her that she loved her a lot and assured her that she will never desert her or let anyone harm her. They hugged each other and cried relentlessly. Karishma also asked for forgiveness for her rude behaviour. The session ended.

However, after the session Karishma had a valid question, "How do I know that what I saw was not my imagination?"

"It's very natural for you to have such a doubt" I said. "Were you aware that your mom was going to undergo an abortion in the third month of pregnancy?"

"No," she answered.

"Well, go back home and ask her if this is true."

That same evening I got a call from Karishma, and she said, "It's a miracle. Each and every detail I saw during my regression was absolutely true. Thank you so much, I feel so relieved now."

She sounded as if a heavy weight was lifted from her soul.

While we are in the foetal state, we are like a sponge. We absorb the emotions of our parents, and other people around us. Medical research has also proven that the mother's state of mind during pregnancy has an effect on the child's emotional, physical and mental well-being. If the mother goes through emotional upheavals, stress or anxiety, it may result in birth complications, premature birth or even miscarriages. On the emotional level, it will instil fear and insecurities in the baby. But when the mother is relaxed and happy, a hormone called oxytocin is released, which helps in smooth delivery and creates the feeling of love and joy. It also increases the immunity of the child. Neurotransmitters moving inside the mother's body due to this release create a chemical and physical imprint on the baby's brain and body. The message imprinted is that there is safety and peace. The baby feels secure and taken care of.

The mental and emotional strength of a child starts building from the foetal stage, when the baby absorbs all the emotions from the mother and the surroundings. Hence it is very important for an expecting mother to be in a happy state of mind. The foundation for the mother-child relationship begins in the womb itself.

Isn't it amazing that apart from past life connections, the soul also starts to develop bonds right from the foetal stage? Relationships and the issues related to it are deeper rooted than they actually seem to be.

Soul mates

Some relations are special. They have a magnetic pull that may supersede logical reasoning, and there is alchemy when two such people come together. This can be experienced in any relationship irrespective of the sex of the two people involved. This may not be a perfect bond, but there is a knowing that they are meant to be with one another. The people may not be physically related, but the bond experienced between them is deep and everlasting. This kind of relationship is apparent between two soul mates.

How do we recognize our soul mates? Every soul longs for the soul companion with whom such an eternal bond can be shared. We come across a lot of people in our life in the form of various relationships but not all can be our soul mates. Some of them are mere karmic relationships.

A strong sign for identifying a soul mate is the feeling of familiarity between two souls, which is mutual. They feel comfortable in each other's presence without the fear of being judged. On meeting a soul mate, a deep and instant connection is set right from the beginning; the sense of calm and knowing experienced cannot be explained in words. There is an upward surge of energy and empowering feeling in each other's presence. There is a feeling of equality and gentleness in the relationship. These relationships take both the souls to a new dimension beyond the physical realm. More than anything, they are best friends and their relationship is centred on love and compassion, with a focus on each other's spiritual development.

All the people closely associated with us during the lifetime are from the same soul group, but all of them need not be our soul mates; although there can be more than one soul mate in a life time. If you feel an invisible pull towards another soul which satisfies the above mentioned criteria, you are fortunate to have found your soul mate.

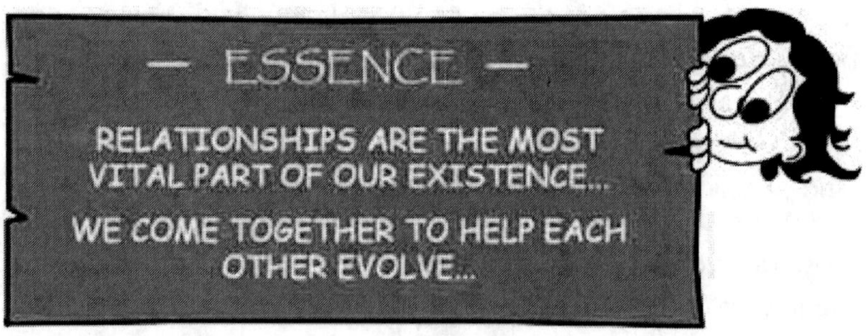

4

WHY DO BAD THINGS HAPPEN TO GOOD PEOPLE?

Ooops...!!

Whatever we give,
universe gives us back,

This law's infallible,
though not in white & black

It also gives us answer to
why do good people,

Have to suffer the pain,
because of nature's smack

"Why do bad things happen to good people?"

This question drove me crazy a few years back.

I know of an old lady in her late 70s, who lives by herself in a spacious apartment in Mumbai's suburbs. She comes across as a very loving and caring person, and never misses an opportunity to help people. She loves cooking and inviting people for dinner at her home. She may not be able to strike an intellectual conversation, but whenever I meet her, I go home wiser. When I met her for the first time I thought, she is one of the blessed ones.

Later, when I learnt what she has gone through in her life, I was stunned. This lady got married at an early age and had four kids – two daughters and two sons. When the youngest son was six, she learnt that her husband had another family and three sons. She was shattered. Her husband, a businessman, used to physically abuse her but she had never told anyone about that, not even her children. She was completely dependent on him financially. She felt powerless in that situation. In the meantime, her elder son went abroad and had no intention of coming back. The youngest son developed serious health issues and passed away. It was really difficult for her to come to terms with all of the tragedy and mishaps in her life. When her younger daughter, a teenager, learnt about her father's other family, she stood by her mother and forced her to leave the house.

The two daughters and mother left the house with her jewellery and her savings without their father's knowledge. They managed to rent a house far away from where they used to live. As she was beginning to roll with the punches, the elder daughter's boyfriend abandoned her and she committed suicide. Now she was left with her only daughter, as the son never kept in touch. But the mother and daughter supported each other to bounce back to life.

It was unbelievable to me that the lady I knew to be always cheerful and positive had been through so much; and the first thought that crossed my mind was, "Why do bad things happen to good people?"

When I tried to sympathize with her, she said, "My life's experiences have shaped me into a better person."

I partially found my answer in her statement.

As mentioned in the earlier chapters, we plan our own challenges before coming to the earth plane, so that we can develop ourselves and climb up the ladder of evolution. But the flipside is that as we grow older, we forget whatever we planned. And when we go through difficult times we wonder, 'God is so unfair, I have never done anything bad to anyone all my life, then why do I have to go through so many problems?'

The answer lies in the theory of karma.

What is karma?

A Sanskrit word that means action, karma is a process of cause and effect which is associated with our thoughts, words and action. The law of karma basically holds that whatever we give comes back to us in manifold; but it may or may not come back from the same person or in the same lifetime. This explains that even if we have not done anything bad to anyone in this lifetime, we may have to experience suffering because of the previous life karmas.

It is important to remember that karma is neither good nor bad. Any thoughts, words or actions that help us to move towards our purpose is good karma; and any thoughts, words or actions that pull us away from our purpose is bad karma for us.

I heard of a story that explains this concept beautifully. There was a saint who lived in a hut in the forest. He spent most of his time meditating under a banyan tree. On one such day, while the saint was meditating, a deer calf that was being chased by a hunter came running to him. Seeing the plight of the deer calf, the saint decided to protect it, and hid it in his hut. The hunter came in search of it soon.

On seeing the saint, he asked, "O wise man, did you see any deer calf passing by?"

"Yes, it has gone to the left," the saint replied.

The hunter thought to himself, 'he looks like a pious man, he will not lie.' He turned to the left, and went off to continue his search.

In the above story, the saint has lied. So will it be a good karma or a bad karma? Well, for the saint, his purpose is to be loving and compassionate towards the living beings. Therefore his speaking a lie will not add to the bad karmas.

Karma teaches us to take responsibility for our actions, and understanding this theory is a major step in our spiritual evolution.

There are two explanations of karma. One is fear-based and holds that - 'whatever you sow, you reap. Karma is the consequence that is brought to you based on your actions, and you are constantly being judged by someone up there.'

The second is love-based – 'Karma is a gift that brings you lessons for your soul's personal growth, and will continue to bring these lessons back around until you have learnt them.'

As per the theory, there are four types of karmas.

Sanchit karma: This is like a complete balance sheet of karmas, collected throughout various lifetimes as humans. We create karmas every moment, through our thoughts, words and deeds. Each karma – good or bad – gets added to this bank of karmas.

Prarabdh karma: These are karmas that have ripened and are ready to fructify. We say that our life unfolds as per our destiny. However as per the law of karma, destiny is nothing but our karmas ready to give fruits. We are governed by two things: the challenges or situations we've planned before coming to this earth, and the karmas created by us when reacting to these situations in all our lifetimes. Whenever we do something good or bad, karma may bring it back in this lifetime itself, or it may get deposited in the karma bank and fructify in another lifetime.

When I was young, I had heard a beautiful story that could help explain Prarabhd karma.

There was a poor lady who was barely able to sustain herself and on a hot summer afternoon, a thirsty young boy came to her door asking for water. The boy was in tatters, and looked very pale. Feeling sympathetic, the lady invited him inside her home, and offered some food and water. The poor young lad, who was famished, ate greedily and she fed him until he was satiated. The boy left her house thanking her for this act of kindness.

After almost 25 years of this incident, the same lady was hospitalized due to some rare illness for which she had to undergo a surgery. At the time of discharge from the hospital, as she went to the counter to settle the bills with her life's savings, the woman at the counter said, "Don't worry ma'am, your bills have been already paid." The lady was shocked. She had nobody in this world who could have paid the hospital bills! Puzzled, she asked, "Could you please tell me who settled my bills?" The woman at the counter said, "I am sorry ma'am, that person didn't disclose his name, but has left a note for you."

The note read, "A small gesture for the act of kindness you showed 25 years ago. Had you not fed me then, I wouldn't have seen this day. I owe my life to you!"

This is how Prarabdh karma works. Strangely though, sometimes people who are not even related to us in this birth, miraculously come forward to help us, when we need it the most.

Agami karma: The karmas that are created every moment by our thoughts, words and deeds, and are constantly being added to the Sanchit karma, are called Agami karma. For example, if we are performing an act of kindness today, it gets credited to our Sanchit karma only to be debited once it is ready to fructify.

Kriyaman karma: The karma that isn't added to Sanchit karma, but is settled immediately is called Kriyaman karma. Here you see an instant result. You don't have to wait for the karma to bear fruit. It resolves itself there and then. For example, you do something wrong and you are immediately punished, or you do a good deed and get instantly rewarded for the same.

Our lives are completely governed by our karmas and they teach us or reward us.

Untimely deaths

Recently, a close friend lost her teenage son to an inexplicable fever. The whole family was inconsolable and it took them a lot of time and strength to accept his passing. Occasionally they questioned God, 'what did we ever do wrong to deserve this?' And then they felt guilty often, wondering if they had done everything they could to save him. This usually happens in case of untimely deaths. The near and dear ones feel they did not do enough and this feeling often drowns them in an ocean of guilt.

However, we need to understand that each soul in on an individual journey and the time of entry and exit is pre-decided. So we cannot take the blame and responsibility on us.

My friend's family wanted to do a session with me. They were keen to connect and communicate with their son at the soul level. There is a technique in past life regression where one can connect to the departed soul. When the soul leaves the body, it exists on a subtle level and it is possible to connect to this subtle energy by going into the deeper levels of the mind. I was happy to guide them so that they could connect with him to get their answers, and most importantly, overcome the overwhelming guilt they were drowning in. During the session, their son told them that he had moved to a higher dimension and was busy helping other souls in the spirit realm. He was happy there and would take a rebirth after some time. He requested them to move on in their respective lives and also told them that he will support them to achieve their life's purpose.

Our deceased loved ones never really leave us, as all the seven planes are right here. It's just that we can't see them. And when we pass on to the other level after death, we are reunited. Although the time of our birth and death, and our purpose is decided by us in the spirit world, we forget about it as we get immersed in the day to day routine. Slowly, in this gross level of our existence on the earth plane, we get conditioned by the beliefs formed by us and also get influenced by the beliefs of people around us. We slowly start believing that we are the body and get completely immersed in doing only what satiates the needs of the body, getting attached to the people and things around us.

Sickness or disease is just one reason for the soul to leave the body. When the time of death nears, any reason is good enough. In 2006 when serial bomb blasts took place in the local trains in Mumbai, many heart wrenching stories came forth. Some of the regular commuters to work reported that they missed that particular train on the fatal day due to some unavoidable reason and could evade the calamity; but some who became victims accidently boarded the ill-fated train.

Miscarriages and stillborn babies

During the course of pregnancy, moms-to-be undergo common physical and emotional changes that lead up to childbirth, from weight gain to mood swings. The expectant mother forms an emotional bond with the baby right from the foetal stage. Hence it is a big blow to the mother and the family in case of a miscarriage or if the baby is stillborn. However, if we look at the whole situation from the perspective of evolution, things will look quite different than they appear.

The reasons for miscarriages and the birth of stillborn can be any of the following:

- the soul is left with a few karmas to complete with the mother
- there is an important lesson of detachment to be learnt in such a case
- the soul feels that the conditions are yet not conducive for its growth

Many times it is found that soul then comes back to the same parents later as their next child.

One needs to develop a higher perspective of looking at the situations and challenges in life. By doing so, one can accelerate the soul's spiritual growth.

Suicides

In case of suicides, a person who is dejected or depressed decides to take life in his or her own hands. In such situations, even if the soul realises its mistake immediately, the body is no longer suitable for the soul to return back to. Since it is an untimely death, the soul is left in limbo and not allowed to cross over to the other side till the decided time of exit. The soul has to spend the remaining lifespan on the earth plane without a body. As per the universal law, we have no right to take what we cannot give. Life is one such thing. Taking one's own life is not only a legal offence but also a karmic one.

If we understand life from the perspective of the soul's evolution process and karmas, we will come out of the duality of good and bad. Once we understand that every small thing happening in our life is helping us move ahead in the process of evolution, we will be grateful for even the so called bad things that happen to us.

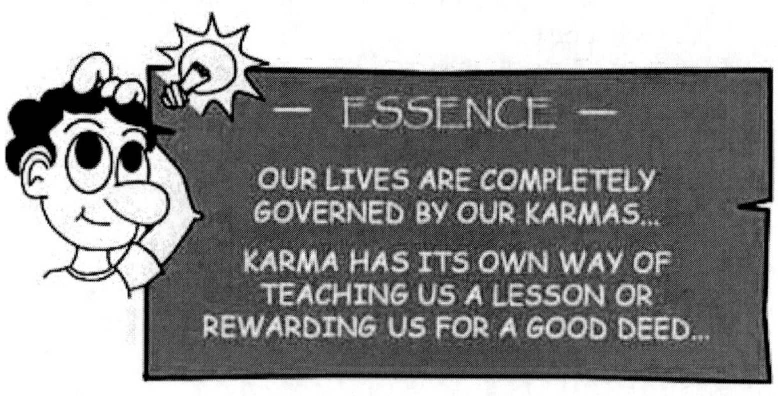

5

WHY DO I EXPERIENCE REPETITIVE PATTERNS?

NOT
AGAIN !!
WHAT'S THE
OPPOSITE OF
'EUREKA'... ??

5

Many times we feel stuck,
in patterns insane
Going through same situations,
again and again
But once we learn the
lessons, and transcend
We can move ahead in life,
and break the chain

When Krish, my friend's son who was studying in Class Five, got his report card, he came to his dad sobbing. "I failed in the exams, Dad. The teacher said that I have to repeat Class Five. All my friends have gone to the next class", he said. I was present there and was curious to see my friend's reaction. I have seen many parents creating a big ruckus about the exam results, as if the whole world has come to a halt. But my friend truly surprised me. He hugged his son and wiping his tears, said, "You know why this happened, Krish? Because you did not learn your lessons properly. Now you know why your mom and I were repeatedly asking you to study. If you don't learn what is being taught to you in school, you will have to repeat your lessons again and again until you learn it well."

Sometimes big things come in small packages. There was a huge learning in the simple statement made by my friend.

As mentioned earlier, according to the theory of evolution, the earth plane is a school and we, as souls, are students. Our life is so designed that we keep experiencing the challenges we have pre-determined for ourselves so as to learn valuable lessons, and transcend them. However, when we fail to learn the lesson, the same situation or challenge will present itself again. The problem starts when we refuse to look at the challenge as a learning curve. Hence it comes back again and again, and we get stuck in a repetitive pattern.

For most people, whenever something negative happens, their first instinct is to brush it off as just a one-off incident or to blame the circumstances. The second time it happens, they may still do the same. When it occurs for the third time, they may think it is a coincidence, but it's beginning to trigger some thought that there might be something that's attracting these situations. After the fourth, fifth or sixth time, it becomes clear that this has become an established pattern.

One of my workshop participants, 50-year-old Smruti told me that everyone in her life had been taking her for granted since childhood.

Sometimes, friend and relatives would just barge into her

house without prior notice, while at times people would make commitments on her behalf, that she was then obliged to fulfil. She never said no to anyone, had lost her voice and was constantly manipulated by everyone, and of course, was miserable about it.

"Why does this happen with me?" was her question.

"What do you think, Smruti?" I asked her,

"Maybe, because I cannot say no when I should" she said, thoughtfully.

"Exactly... You need to stand up for yourself. By letting someone else dictate your life, you are putting them in the driver's seat. Learn to be in charge of your life and see how things change around you," I replied.

When faced with the repetitive patterns in our life, we often question why something is happening to us again and again but most of the time, we get so frustrated with the recurrence of the same event that we fail to acknowledge, understand, accept and integrate the underlying meaning of that pattern.

One morning I got a call from Simran who was desperate for help. We met the next day, and I found her to be very depressed though she was trying hard to hide her true feelings behind the mask of a happy person.

Forty and single, Simran had had two broken relationships in the past, and was going through the third break-up when we met. The common thing about all three men she dated was that they were already married. She wanted to know why she was attracting only relationships, that had no future, into her life.

Many times, such issues are deep-rooted, sometimes in a past life or the past of the present life. To identify the root cause of the issue, it was necessary to dig into the memories of her childhood.

While chatting with Simran, she mentioned an interesting fact. As a child, her mom always told her that her purpose in life was to get married and look after her husband and family. Simran lived under the dominating influence of her mom and always tried to please her. She felt that she was never good enough and went an extra mile to prove herself to others. Unfortunately, her mom passed away, leaving her in despair.

Having developed a low self-esteem, Simran continued to please others seeking appreciation and approval. She surrendered to all the three men in her life and was seeking love and approval from them. These men took advantage of her weakness. By the third relationship, she had formed a belief that she will never find a single man.

The sessions with Simran was focused on helping her regain her self-esteem and delete the negative belief that she attracts only married men. After a few sessions, Simran could come out of this cycle and she has now found the man of her dreams, who she will marry soon.

Sometimes, because of our negative conditioning, we fall into the same trap repeatedly. This needs to be broken. Here, there was an important learning for Simran; to love and accept herself unconditionally.

Many of us get stuck in the predicament of repetitive patterns, which are limiting and constrictive. They also hamper our movement and growth. Some of us are not even aware that this is happening to us; all we can feel are bouts of restlessness, claustrophobia, directionless and lack of joy. And we don't understand why. At this point, we need to learn to operate from our higher self. The repetitive patterns signal us to change the course of our life. The universe has its own ways of communication. When we drift away from the purpose of our life, it tells us through such patterns.

I know a girl who is a gifted painter and has an innate ability to draw and paint human faces, especially the eyes. She hasn't ever been to an art school, but her paintings are par excellence. I was surprised to know that she studied commerce and was preparing for an entrance exam for a company secretary course. She sat for and failed the exam thrice. Once when I met her through a common friend, I could not hold myself back and asked her, "Why do you want to become a company secretary?

You are a gifted painter." She said, "It is my parents' dream that I become a company secretary. But I am really not interested in it. My first love is painting. When I am engaged in painting, I forget everything." Her passion is art, the universe is giving her enough signals to change her path, but she is simply not able to fathom the signs. Every time, she appears for the exam and fails. The result is that she is now depressed.

Understanding our own selves and knowing our purpose can help a great deal in breaking the repetitive patterns in our life. If we ever catch ourselves in a loop, then it is time to pause and reflect.

Patterns occur as a result of the internal, fundamental frameworks we live by, which refer to the inner beliefs and values we hold. To get rid of these repetitive behaviors, we need to look inward, examine what triggers them, uncover the underlying causes and resolve them at the root level.

Once this is done, one can experience a sense of freedom and empowerment and change the course of destiny in the positive direction.

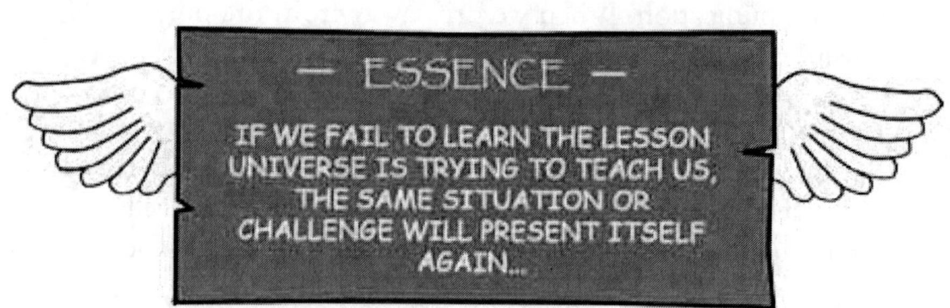

6

WHY AM I UNHAPPY?

SALES
THIS YEAR...
INSTEAD OF BONUS
WE ARE GIVING
SPECIAL REWARDS

6

Happiness is really our basic nature,
our own part
We are here to celebrate,
and follow our heart
If you feel unhappy, then stop
and think for a while
Perhaps you need to give your life,
a fresh new start

Our life as a human being can be beautifully depicted as a chariot, drawn by five horses, driven by a charioteer and there is one passenger on board. The chariot represents our body, which is a vehicle, meant to carry the passenger, our soul, to the desired destination. The charioteer is our intellect, steering the horses, which represent our emotions. Whether the passenger reaches the destination will depend on how well the charioteer controls the reins of the horses and directs them.

Here are some common problems that I have seen my clients, or people in my life face that we have all faced at some point or the other.

Unresolved emotions

Emotions are nothing but e-motion, i.e. energy in motion. This energy is so strong that it can drive us in any direction and how we move ahead in life depends on how well the intellect controls our emotions. Negative emotions such as anger, guilt, regret, jealousy, fear, anxiety etc. pull us back from our path.

My dad, who is now 88-year-old, often narrates an incident that happened 65 years ago, and invariably, whenever he does, his eyes are filled with tears even today.

He remembers the day he graduated and came home, triumphant, with his degree. It was as if he had won the world, because earning a bachelor's degree was a great achievement in the 1940s. His mother, proud of her son's achievement, was eagerly waiting for him at the door.

"As soon as I arrived home," my dad says. "I threw my bag on one side, and straightaway went to change my clothes, completely ignoring my mom. She had cooked my favourite dish and planned to have dinner with me. But I was so preoccupied with my accomplishment that I did not pay any heed to her, and went out for dinner with my friends. I later learnt that my mom was so hurt by my behaviour that she slept without eating that night. It was her magnanimity that she did not even mention it the next day. When I learnt about this, my heart just crumbled under the heavy load of guilt and regret."

My grandmother passed away a few years after this incident took place, but the guilt and regret have remained in my dad till date.

The memory of this incident makes him really sad but he has to let go of the baggage he's been carrying for the past 65 years, in order to be happy in life. His mother must have forgiven him and forgotten about it after a while, but he has not forgiven himself.

Inexplicable emotional issues

Kaushal, a 55-year-old professional, came to me with the problem of irrational anger. He told me that he would lose his temper with anyone over the smallest things, without really being able to justify it. This was adversely affecting his life and relationships with his dear ones. He understood that his anger was irrational and illogical, but was helpless; he desperately wished to change.

When I regressed him, he went into a life in an olden Indian era. He saw himself as a woman married into an orthodox family. Her husband and in-laws always troubled her, citing the insufficient dowry her parents offered. The dowry system was very prevalent at that time. After a lot of physical, mental and emotional torture, one day she was doused in kerosene and burnt alive. In tremendous pain, and enraged, she screamed helplessly, pleading for someone to save her, but nobody did. Finally, she succumbed to death, and died angry, which manifested itself in this life as unresolved anger.

During the session, after he re-lived that life, I guided Kaushal to the LBL state where, under the guidance of the ascended masters, he was asked to forgive those people who were responsible for the girl's death. It took great effort and persuasion for him to do so but later, Kaushal slowly found a remarkable change in his temper.

Living with the hurts of the past

The pent-up emotions, if not resolved from time to time, not only affect us in this lifetime but also get carried forward to future lives. Similarly, our mental, emotional and physical well-being can be attributed to how well we have been able to deal with the past. Many people say, "What is the need to look into the past? One should always move ahead." I completely agree. But I also feel it is of utmost importance to heal the past as well. Though the past exists only in our memories, it forms an integral part of our soul. The unresolved emotions from our past act as roadblocks, preventing us from moving ahead in life. This, at times, becomes a reason for our unhappiness.

I knew Celina and her family for a while, and when I met her in Goa a few years ago, found her to be in depression; this shocked me because I had never even suspected such a thing. Celina is a successful doctor, is married and has a son and a daughter. Her husband is loving and supportive and the kids are intelligent and talented. She had a picture-perfect life that anyone could be envious of, but she was unhappy.

"I don't know why, but I hate my husband and my son. In fact, I hate all the men in my life and I feel miserable about it," she confessed. Clearly, she needed help and after speaking with her, I realized that she is entangled in lot of self-created issues. To get to the root of the problem, I realized she needed a present life regression.

I was stunned at how a deep-rooted memory, which had been consciously forgotten, surfaced during the session. This is what Celina described to me:

When she was four years old, she was travelling in a local bus with her mom. Since the bus was crowded, and Celina was in her mom's arms, a man sitting on the window seat offered to take Celina on his lap. Thinking that she would be comfortable there, her mother gave her to the man. After some time, Celina found herself in the tight clutches of this man, unable to move. He molested her. Celina had to struggle for a long time, to free herself from his clutches and go back to her mom.

This incident left such a deep impact on her psyche, that as she grew up she started hating all men. Since the memory was brought to her conscious awareness, it was processed and released from her deep subconscious mind. This was followed by a few counselling sessions. There was a gradual positive change in Celina after every session. She seemed to be happier than before, after letting go of what she was unknowingly holding on to. She also began to feel grateful for the blessings in her life.

It is amazing at how memories that we think are forgotten, affect us without being consciously aware of it. Though it may not seem so, the root cause of unhappiness in the present moment can sometimes be rooted in the past.

Fears and anxieties about the future

We feel anxious about our future most of the times, and worry about our professional and personal lives constantly. These insecurities and worries contribute to the unhappiness in our life and since they are the projections of our mind, we must keep these negative feelings at bay. Understanding and trusting the larger plan that life has for each of us, allows us to understand why every event occurs and this realization helps us pull ourselves out of any unhappy situation.

Trying to find happiness outside of ourselves

Most often, we feel happy only if something 'good' happens in

our life. This means that our happiness is dependent on external events. We believe that happiness is a random and fleeting feeling but if we understand the universal plan and how we have evolved till the present lifetime, we will not feel the same. Our soul is absolutely unique, and we need to connect to that core of ourselves; once we do, we will feel connected to the whole universe and understand that everything is connected. Thus, we will be always happy.

Numerous people are focused on gathering wealth and material things, which may provide a temporary boost of happiness, but then we quickly become bored. The more we collect, the more the desire grows but the more we try to find real happiness in these things, the more it will evade us. Because true happiness comes from within, and not from outside of ourselves. During the process of our evolution, we spend many lifetimes in learning this fact but the sooner we understand this process, the faster we come out of this pattern.

Unchanging circumstances

There might be times when we feel there's nothing going on in our life, or nothing new is happening. The same old patterns keep repeating themselves. We feel uninspired, like we are victims of our circumstances, and label life as flat and meaningless. In such situations, we must go deeper and ask ourselves, what is the real meaning or purpose behind this state? Once that question is asked, the universe makes sure we get our answer.

Constant comparison

The more we define our happiness by how other people look, what they have achieved, or what they own, the unhappier we become. Once we understand the process of reincarnation, we understand that each one of us is a different soul on his or her own journey of evolution, and we are each exactly where we are supposed to be in this process; the larger plan of the universe is always unfolding in our lives. We must realize that our basic and prime responsibility is towards our own journey and development.

Feeling of worthlessness

Another interesting fact is that the people present at the time of the birth of a child, contribute a lot to building up the self-esteem of the child. The feelings of rejection, love or hate are instilled at that stage and these go a long way in shaping the personality of that soul. A feeling of worthlessness can lead to being in a state of unhappiness most of the time. If you don't feel happy about yourself, how can you feel good about the world?

A girl who came to me for counselling suffered from very

low self-esteem. After talking to her, I found out that she was the third girl child in the family. When she was conceived everyone, including the parents, was expecting a baby boy, and was disappointed when a girl was born. The mother refused to even touch the child for two days. Can you imagine the trauma that little baby must have gone through, and the feelings of rejection fear and worthlessness she experienced? Similar to the foetal state, a new-born baby is also like a sponge, which is always absorbing the emotions of the parents and everyone else around.

This girl, while growing up, always tried to please everyone around her and in the process lost her identity, which made her very unhappy.

The important fact one needs to understand is that every soul comes on this earth with a specific purpose and equally contributes in the evolution of mankind as a whole. No person is insignificant or worthless. It is just our perspective of looking at things that make it good or bad.

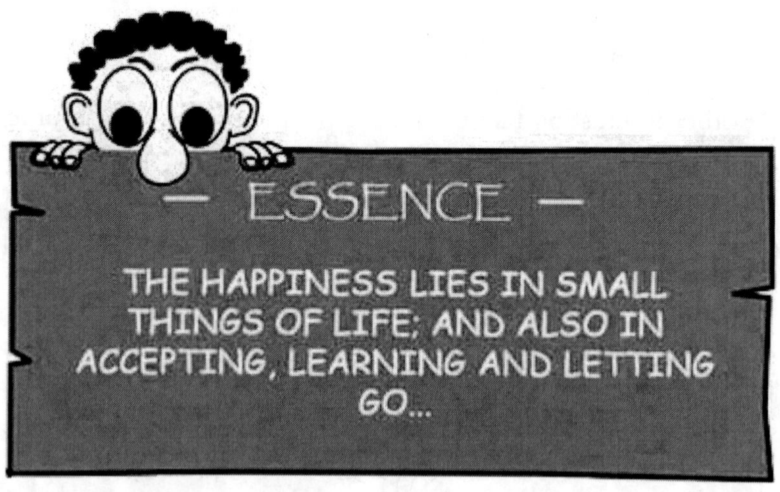

7

WHY IS THERE SO MUCH DISPARITY IN THE WORLD?

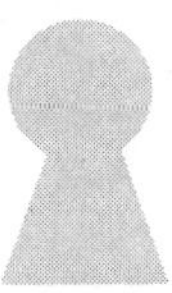

I USED TO OWN THIS PLACE...
BEFORE THE STOCK MARKET CRASH...

7

We are on our own journey,
towards our goal

Each one of us in unique,
and a divine soul

We may be at different
levels of evolution

But primarily we are all one,
and part of the whole

What is your reaction when you see a beggar on the street, running on his crutches from one car to the next, begging for alms? Do you feel sad, or sympathetic? Do you wonder why this disparity exists between a homeless man and the one living in a mansion? If, on one hand, we are taught that we are all the children of one God, then why does God Himself treat everyone differently? One child gets all the riches in life while the other child of the same God, has to toil to get even one square meal. Isn't this a great disparity? Isn't this a biased approach of God towards His own children?

Since I was highly sensitive by nature, these questions really troubled me. There was a time when I saw a beggar eating food from a dustbin, and I lost my appetite for several days. Of course, I was grateful for what I had and that I could have the food of my choice every day, but still the question remained – why can't some people even have the basic necessities of life, while others live in abundance?

As I started delving deeper into this subject, I realized there is disparity in the world not only in the material sense but also in terms of thoughts, faith, and deeds. For example, a small child can be more mature and understanding than an 80-year-old. In several parts of India, in a few remote villages, women can't leave their house unless they are escorted by a male member of the family and they have to keep their faces veiled at all times, while in the cities, women rightfully wear whatever they want and travel by themselves fearlessly.

Seeing disparity in every walk of life literally drove me crazy for many years, until I found some convincing answers in the theory of evolution. I came across an interesting premise that proved to be useful in answering these questions. During the process of evolution, a soul goes through various stages. We, as souls, start our journey on the earth plane first as rocks, minerals and crystals, then evolve into plants and trees, then into sea creatures, followed by land creatures. After experiencing animal lives, we finally step into human life. Until the animal stage, our evolution is natural, as an automatic process. As soon as we become humans, we are given an additional faculty to help us make decisions – our intellect. We are given the power to choose. At the same time, we are also given an additional responsibility, in the form of karma. From human life onwards we start contributing towards the process of evolution.

Once in human phase, the soul goes through six stages of evolution, before mixing back with the source. These stages are also seen as the steps to evolution.

Infant soul:

The souls who have just come into human lives are infant souls. As the name suggests, it is a very nascent stage. At this stage, the soul is new to the concept of human life. It is inexperienced, hence full of fears and insecurities. While in animal stage, the highest learning is survival. In the final stages of animal life, the soul is close to humans, mostly as pets or domesticated animals. At human stage, the soul starts the journey with survival as the basic instinct. At the infant soul stage, the soul also likes to be away from social life, and is happy to be alone. These souls may be labelled as simpleton by others, as they are just eating, sleeping and living a basic life. They are often perceived by others as being childish, innocent and ignorant to the complexities of life. Possessing a very simplistic understanding of life, and a genuinely guileless approach to the world, these souls shy away from any kind of civilized life. Because they lack both social understanding and self-inhibition, they are capable of committing antisocial or immoral acts without any sense of wrongdoing. While infant souls may lack the moral principles, social grace and cultural understanding of older souls; they are actually completely innocent beings without pretence or agenda.

Baby soul:

This is the next in the stage of evolution. After spending several lifetimes as infant souls, and getting a feel of the human life, the soul graduates to the baby soul level. After grounding itself in human civilization, as a baby soul, its life heavily revolves around finding the belonging and security. The baby soul likes to live a very disciplined and structured life abiding by rules and regulations. Souls who are at the baby soul stage understand only good or bad, or right or wrong. For them everything is black and white. No grey areas in between. The desire to follow a structured life makes them rigid. They are driven by 'exercising the duty and that what is right'. If they deviate from their structured path, they feel immense guilt and are unable to handle it. In a nutshell, baby souls are super conservative, orthodox, moralistic, religiously devout, and great followers.

Young soul:

Till this stage the soul learns how to survive and live a structured life. Now is the time for the soul to experience the influence of wealth, power, fame, and material and physical pleasure. In this stage, the soul tends to be ambitious, materialistic, competitive, and worldly. A young soul is greatly motivated by financial success and finer aspects of life. This is the third stage of evolution where the soul starts exploring and expressing individuality and discovering the power of independence in thoughts and action. The focus is completely outward and there is a strong tendency to compare one with others on materialistic possessions. They also evaluate their self worth based on their achievements.

For a young soul, success can become more important than anything else, including happiness and relationships. Young souls have an ego-driven personality, keen to prove themselves in the world at large. They like to think for themselves, assert their own opinions, follow their own agenda, and feel their way is superior to others. They are generally attracted to some form of worldly success - fame, fortune, power, or glory. In fact, they are more fearful of death and losing their possessions than souls at other stages.

Mature soul:

By this stage, the soul has an understanding that happiness cannot be found outside and essentially has to be searched within. Mature souls tend to be thoughtful, reflective and sincere within themselves, and sensitive and empathetic towards others. Their awareness is no longer egocentric. They have a desire to transcend the ego, and to be more authentic. This creates a rift internally and makes life much more complicated and overwhelming. The soul develops a larger perspective towards life, reinventing and accommodating.

This is the stage when the genuine search for real truth starts. At this stage the soul starts asking the fundamental questions such as 'who am I?', 'why am I here?' or 'what is the purpose of my life?'. The mature soul makes an attempt to understand its relationship with the universe and with people around; and hence goes through emotional intensities. Mature souls tend to do a lot of soul searching. This can be one of the most challenging and tiring stages in the process of evolution.

Old soul:

Old souls tend to radiate some degree of depth and wisdom that cannot be missed. Having moved beyond the stage of conflicts and emotional intensities, they are also lighter and have a sense of joyous freedom. They seem to enjoy the freedom of being very much in the world, but not of it. The old souls are relatively calm and compassionate towards other living beings and are somewhat detached. At this stage, the soul begins to understand self and the purpose of its existence on earth. An old soul understands that it is a part of the whole and respects each fellow being the way they are without being judgmental. At this stage the soul reaches the higher level of understanding, slowly nearing its highest goal. The old soul is not interested in success or fame so much, as doing something it loves well, and finding inner satisfaction. They tend to go their own unique way in life, letting go and letting be. They seem to live life in a detached way that may seem very weird and eccentric to younger souls. The old soul comes to perceive everything, as part of one great tapestry. Towards the end of the stage, there may be more emphasis on teaching rather than simply learning: passing on the lessons learnt and showing others the way.

Transcendental soul:

This is the final stage, just before completing the human phase or attaining *moksha* or *nirvana*. At this stage the soul is ready to come out of life and death cycle, and mix back with the source. It understands the purpose, the process of evolution and the fact that each one of us is a part of the same source. In this stage, the soul begins to spread this wisdom to the masses. The transcendental souls, dedicate their lives to bring about great social changes and spread the understanding.

Infinite soul:

An infinite soul is the incarnation of the divine source in human form. They are the co-creators in the creative process of the universe and are also known as avatars. Infinite souls take physical manifestation only once in many centuries or millenniums.

A soul spends several lifetimes in each stage as it spirals upward. The stages up to the transcendental soul has further seven levels, during which the soul goes from initiation to mastery and integration of that stage. For example, as an Infant soul, the basic learning is survival. Therefore, the soul keeps taking birth in this stage until it masters the purpose or learning of that stage, which is survival.

The number of lifetimes in each level depends on the soul and how quickly it wants to learn the lessons and move on. The soul can move from one level to another in the same lifetime as well.

The interesting part is that in each of the stages, the soul goes through four different types of lives repeatedly. These four types are broadly classified as the life of a Prince, Peasant, Prostitute and Priest, and are also known as four 'P's in the process of evolution. These are the lives the soul chooses as per the process of evolution and the challenges it is looking at, for its own development.

A life of **Prince**, means a life of abundance, where one experiences prosperity. There's no scarcity in this life type. However, there are other challenges that come along with this kind of life. One can learn the virtue of kindness and gratitude, among other things.

The life of **Peasant** is a complete contrast to the life of Prince, and here one has to go through immense poverty. The soul in this lifetime chooses very poor parents and circumstances. One can learn acceptance and faith, among other things during this type of life.

In a **Prostitute** life, one seeks sensual pleasures. One may be a drug addict or an alcoholic, or a prostitute in the literal sense. The important lesson to be learnt is self-control during this type of life.

The life of **Priest** involves being a holy person or teacher. This life is mostly used to gain awareness and understanding.

All these lives are chosen by us with their inherent challenges, with guidance from our master in the LBL state. We also keep shuffling between two or more types of lives in one lifetime. For example, we may be born as peasant but later on becomes a prince or vice-versa.

Most people find this to be a very satisfactory explanation that throws some light on why there is so much disparity in the world. A beggar on the street would have probably chosen that life for the soul's own development, or someone very rich and powerful may lack the wisdom, or a small child may have the intelligence and acumen to understand the deeper secrets of life. Whatever the stage or the type of life the soul chooses, it has to successfully pass through the challenges of that lifetime to evolve to the next level Since we all are on our own soul journey and carrying the baggage of our own karmas, it is unfair to be judgmental about the other souls. That soul may be at a different level of evolution, hence may act or live in a particular way that may not resonate with the other.

During one of my workshops, a lady came to me and said that she had lot of problems in her life. She was so frustrated that she asked me, "Look at my own younger sister. She is living like a princess and here I am, struggling till now for every small thing. Am I never going to see the brighter side of life? Why do I have to go through this?" She did believe in past life regression and hence wanted to find the answers for herself.

In the workshop, she saw a past life in the 1850s, when she was a princess of an Indian kingdom. She led an envious and royal life, full of abundance, and had no reason to complain. Coincidently, she saw her present sister as one of her maids, whom she was close to. This maid was very poor and faced several challenges in her life. After seeing this lifetime and developing a higher understanding, she vowed not to complain and decided to face every challenging situation positively.

If a soul chooses a life of poverty, it is for its own development. But as per the theory mentioned above, once the lesson is learnt, the soul can move from poverty to abundance in the same life itself.

During one of my workshops in New Delhi, one of the participants was a staunch follower of his faith. Since the workshop took place on 25th December, I proposed to take up a meditation on Christ Consciousness on the start of the second day. This man was visibly upset by my proposal and he expressed his displeasure about the same. However, the session of past life regression that we had after lunch miraculously changed his perspective. He was astonished and speechless at the vivid visuals he saw during the session. He went into a past life during which he saw himself in London, as a priest named Andrew. His entire life revolved around Church and it was a very happy and satisfying lifetime.

They say that the Universe gives you answers at the right time and when you are ready for it. In that one session of regression during the workshop, he got some astounding revelations that completely changed him as a person. That is the beauty of PLR.

The process of past life regression gives us a higher perspective on a lot of things, including the divisions between religions. When we see that we have gone through various lifetimes practicing various faiths, we come out of this duality. If each one of us can adopt this view, the world would be a much happier and peaceful place.

PLR is a marvellous tool that helps calm the storm within. It gives a deeper understanding about life, thus aiding the process of evolution. Actually, what we call disparity only exists in our mind; each soul is on an individual journey at different stages of evolution, and hence at the right place.

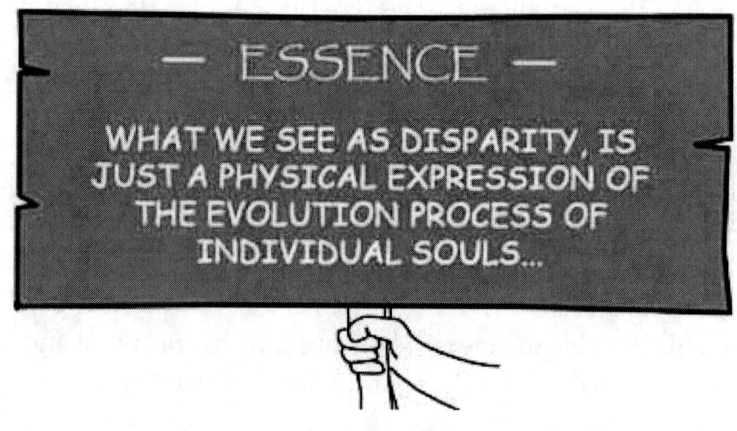

8

WHY DO SOME PEOPLE HAVE IRRATIONAL FEARS AND PHOBIAS?

HE SAYS
HE HAS
FEAR OF
WATER
SO
???

8

What are the things that really scare you,

Or any unfounded fear, that turns you blue?

To find the real reason, you need to dig deep,

Perhaps your previous lives can give you the clue...

Almost a decade ago, when I was working with a multinational company, my job entailed a lot of travel across the globe. Since I love visiting places, exploring different cultures and meeting new people, I enjoyed every bit of this opportunity. Until, on one dreadful day, when I flew from Mumbai to Delhi. As I boarded the plane, something shifted within me and I suddenly started feeling suffocated. I walked to my seat in the business class, still very restless, and sat down, trying not to focus on what I was feeling. My breathing had completely lost its rhythm and my heart was working harder to pump blood. "Something's not right with me," I realized. The two-hour flight seemed never-ending and as the plane landed in Delhi, I was the first one standing at the exit. I was desperate to get out of the plane and breathe fresh air.

This was the first time something like this happened to me.

I was booked in an executive suite at Hyatt in Delhi. But as I entered and looked around the room, I started feeling uneasy again. The executive suite at this hotel, according to many, is particularly spacious. But apparently, it was not spacious enough to calm my nerves.

I dialled the reception and asked to see a doctor. After asking me a few questions and a thorough examination, the doctor diagnosed my condition as anxiety disorder. He prescribed an anti-anxiety pill so that I could get some rest. Nothing helped and I ended up spending half the night in the hotel's lobby, as it was impossible for me to stay in the room. After my meeting the next day, I returned home to Mumbai, completely distressed.

The feeling of suffocation that I experienced in an enclosed space gave rise to panic and then the fear that 'I would die'. This fear manifested in my body in the form of increased palpitations, panting and weakness. My family physician prescribed a few tests to reach to the exact cause of these anxiety attacks, but everything was normal. He concluded my condition as claustrophobia and put me on anti-anxiety drugs. The frequency of these episodes increased, however, and started affecting my professional as well as personal life adversely.

"Why did I suddenly develop claustrophobia out of nowhere?" the question haunted me. However, I needed an immediate solution to my problem more than the answer. Lot of personal research and advice from mentors slowly led me to past life regression therapy, which eventually provided a key to my problem.

During a regression process, I slipped into an immediate past life where I saw myself as a black coal miner in South Africa. Coincidently, in the present life, I was handling coal marketing for a company and we procured a lot of coal from South Africa. In that life, I worked in the coal mines and lead a life of penury with a huge family to take care of. In the form of vivid visuals, I could see my entire life, right from childhood. In the process that lasted for almost two hours, I went back and forth through that lifetime, reliving all the major events.

While experiencing this, I reached a moment where I started feeling anxiety, the same way I felt earlier. I was reliving a traumatic experience of that life. One day while I was working in a coal mine with my colleagues, there was sudden chaos and people started running helter-skelter. I could hear a lot of noises and screams and realized that the whole mine was getting filled with water. We all were running towards the entrance trying to save ourselves. It was dark and I just could not see the way ahead. I panicked. I was short of breath. I started screaming, "Help! Help!" Just as I tried hard to move forward, I realized my feet were stuck and I could not move. Slowly the water level started rising. It was impossible for me breathe. "I am going to die!" was the last thought, before I fell unconscious.

Incidentally, after some time when I opened my eyes, I was still alive. A co-miner had dragged me outside. After a few days of medical care, I recovered physically, but life was never the same after this dreadful incident. It left a very deep scar on my psyche.

I could not believe what I saw. There were striking similarities in both the lives. However, past life regression gave me some amazing answers to my current life situation, particularly about where this claustrophobia came from. Another interesting revelation was that my age of experiencing the phobia the first time in this life matched uncannily with age I was when the coal mine accident took place in the previous lifetime.

The most interesting outcome of the whole regression process was that my claustrophobia disappeared as inexplicably as it had appeared.

A phobia can be described as an irrational fear that leads to anxiety disorder. Depending on what phobia it is, any external or internal factor can act as a trigger. This fear becomes very large in the mind but may not actually exist in real life. Even so, the phobia can affect the normal functioning of a human being and completely mess up anybody's life. Common symptoms of a phobia are palpitations, breathlessness, hot flashes or cold chills, to name a few.

Many of us live with a lot of fears and phobias, for which there are no logical or medical explanations. A fear may form such an integral part of us that we feel it is okay to live with, even though we try to dissociate ourselves from the trigger. For example, if someone suffers from hydrophobia (fear of water), that person will try and stay away from water. If someone has acrophobia (fear of heights), that person will avoid going to places that are at a height. But we don't realize that in the bargain we are missing on so many beautiful aspects of life. As in my case, I loved travelling but after experiencing claustrophobia for the first time, I started avoiding long trips.

One could develop numerous irrational fears and when exposed to the source of the fear, there is a sensation of uncontrollable anxiety. The anxiety is so overwhelming, that the person is unable to stay calm. It is common for sufferers to acknowledge that their fears are irrational, unreasonable and exaggerated; however, in spite of this, they are unable to control their feelings. Hence, it is necessary to go to the root cause. When we re-live the incident by accessing the memory (from where the fear originates) from our subconscious mind, experience the feelings in totality and let go with a higher understanding, the fear itself disappears.

It is observed that the emotions at the time of sudden death in one life get transferred to the next lives. During my practice as a past life regression therapist, I have come across interesting facts like, the fear at the time of death might also manifest in the form of a physical ailment. For example, if someone has died by drowning in water, it may manifest as asthma in the current life; a person who died from burns person may develop skin problems. Though these observations cannot be generalized, it is interesting to note, how the so-called irrational fears and phobias can be deep rooted. We call them irrational because there is no logical or scientific reason for it in the present lifetime. But they are certainly an unresolved part of us. Even if we experience a small fear we should not shy away from confronting it. In PLR parlance, it may me just be a deep-rooted memory of past life or the past of this life, waiting to be released.

One of my clients, Seema came to me to talk about her acrophobia. During our conversation, I realized that though she was an intelligent and ambitious girl, she was not able to scale heights even in her career. She had this deeply embedded fear that she will fall down.

When I regressed her to get to the root cause of her issue, she very easily went to one of her past lives where she saw herself as a simple poor girl living in a small village. She had a step-mother (who coincidently, she identified as her mother in this life), who always ill-treated her. Her father, who was submissive by nature, silently watched her suffer. (Seema identified her father in that lifetime as one of her maternal uncles in the current life). Their village was located on top of a hill, with a breath-taking view of the valley. Whenever she felt sad, Seema would sit at the edge of the hill for hours; just being in nature would wash away all her pain, and she would feel rejuvenated to take life in its stride. One such day while she was standing at the edge of the hill, engrossed in her own thoughts, somebody pushed her from behind. Seema fell in the valley hit her head on a bolder and died instantly.

When her soul left her body, she saw that all the villagers had gathered around her body. At that stage she realized that it was her step-mother who pushed her down the hill and made the whole thing look like a suicide.

The fear of falling down from a height, which got associated with her in that life, surfaced in the current life. So much so, that unknowingly she stopped herself from rising up the career ladder as well. Seema also mentioned that she shared a very sour relationship with her mother of this life and had no attachment with the maternal uncle either.

In Seema's case, death was so sudden, that the soul was traumatized and before even experiencing the feelings, or coming to terms with the situation, was out of the body. Even the fear experienced at the time of falling, got buried within. Since it was a sudden death, it was difficult for the soul to accept everything and move on, so these feelings got carried forward into a future life. During our session, I helped Seema relive the whole incident again, experiencing the fear while falling down, accepting the untimely death, forgiving her parents for their act and letting go or releasing the whole incident. Once this process was complete, Seema had closure, and she felt lighter and more peaceful. The bonus of this therapy is that Seema has now risen to an enviable position in her organization. She no longer fears falling down. Through this therapy, we not only get answers to our 'whys', but it also helps us uproot the problem from its source.

During a workshop, where I conduct group regressions, one of the participants was suffering from an acute case of claustrophobia and after the second session, she shared an interesting experience.

She was born in a strict, orthodox Jewish family in Hungary. She lived in a comfortable home, in a community where people of different religions and backgrounds lived harmoniously, side by side. In 1944, the Germans invaded Hungary. Within a couple of weeks, the Jews were rounded up and sent to ghettos. After two weeks in the ghetto, people were taken to a deserted station where they were packed into cattle wagons and sent to concentration camps. She saw her family and thousands of other Jews being helped from the wagons by men in striped uniforms and being made to wait in a queue. Her family was separated. Her father was taken from the family first, then she and her sister were led one way; their mother and two younger sisters went in a different direction. She learnt that her mother and sisters had been taken to the gas chambers.

She and her sister had their clothes taken away, their hairs shaved off, and were issued camp uniform. They were taken to work in a slave labour camp in Germany. There, she was caught trying to run away. Then as punishment, she was buried alive.

This gave her claustrophobia in the present life, due to which she could not travel even in elevators, but the problem was resolved after the group regression session, in which she released this memory.

In yet another case, a doctor would get frequent nightmares in which all his loved ones were dying in front of him and he was helpless. He would frantically wake up in the middle of night, sweating and feeling suffocated, and go to check if everyone was all right. He was unable to sleep thereafter. This took a toll on his life. It was a recurring phenomenon and he had sleepless nights. Being a doctor, he tried treating himself, but without success and it took him quite some time to believe in PLR. I conducted a couple of sessions with him just to explain what past life regression is all about and how it could possibly help him. When he was willing to try it out, I decided to go ahead with a session. I presumed that it would take a couple of sessions for the doctor to completely come out of this miserable situation.

When I regressed him, he went into a life where he saw himself inside a bungalow engulfed in fire. People tried to save him, but unfortunately he died. He just had a short glimpse of that before I guided him to move on from that life, he went into another past life where he was a farmer who had a huge family. He was poor and could hardly make two ends meet. During this lifetime, he saw all his family members dying before him including his children and wife. It was heartbreaking to see his loved ones pass by in front of his eyes. He felt miserable at being helpless about it. After that he led a lonely life for very long and died at an old age with nobody around him. This feeling of being left alone and his dear ones dying before him, instilled a fear which came in this life and robbed him of his peace.

During the session, in the LBL state, he had a beautiful experience in which he saw his guiding angel turning into the rainbow colours and covering his whole body. He felt the reassurance and the peace he had never experienced before. He was dazed after he came out of the deep trance and truly amazed at what he saw.

Though he did see a relevant past life, he did not get any direct answers to his problems and was, therefore, unsure of the outcome of whole therapy. I assured him that he would be alright after the session but may require a few more sessions. A week passed by and there was no response. I was eagerly awaiting feedback from the doctor. This left me a little anxious. After about three weeks of the session, one morning when I reached out for my mobile phone, there was a message from the doctor. I hurriedly opened the inbox. "You won't believe it, but since our regression session, I have been sleeping like a log. No nightmares, no choking and suffocation, and very peaceful sleep. Most importantly I wake up fresh in the morning and am able to focus on my work in a much better way. Thanks a million Santosh."

I smiled and said to myself, "Why won't I believe this?" Just one session had done the magic.

— ESSENCE —

OUR FEARS AND PHOBIAS MAY JUST BE DEEP-ROOTED MEMORIES OF PAST LIFE OR THE PAST OF PRESENT LIFE, WAITING TO BE RELEASED...

9

WHY DO SOME PEOPLE HAVE OCD?

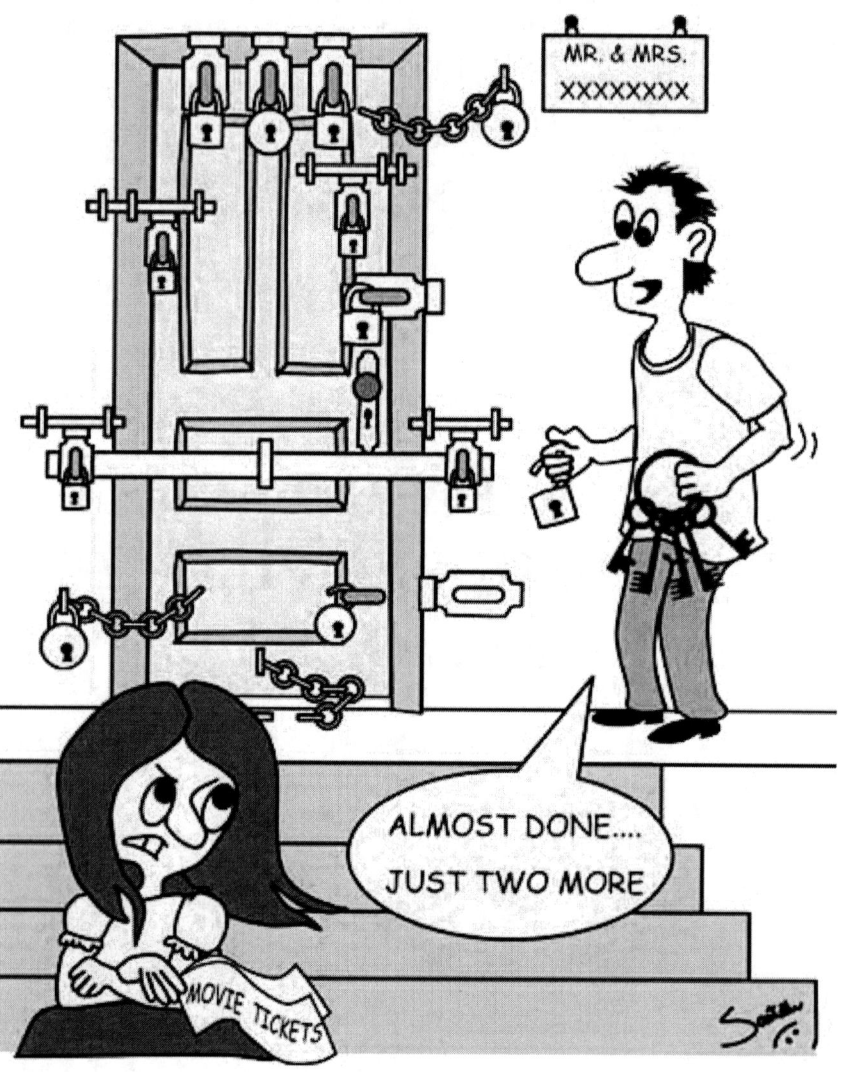
MR. & MRS.
XXXXXXXX
ALMOST DONE....
JUST TWO MORE
MOVIE TICKETS

9

Our habits and our traits,
are residues of our past
That sometimes fade away,
but sometimes do last
Although we all come from the
same source, however
More than symmetry in life,
there's beauty in contrast

When I was a young boy, we once had some family friends over for dinner. On the dinner table, I noticed that the gentleman was very restless. Neither was he enjoying the meal nor the conversation. His wife was trying hard to make up for her husband's disinterest. After a while it became very obvious and my dad asked his friend, "Are you ok? You seem quite restless." Before he could speak his wife replied, "He is too worried about whether he has locked the house properly or not, though he checked it himself several times. He wanted to go and check when we came almost half way. I didn't allow it, hence he is restless."

I giggled at this unexpected reply. It sounded very funny to me at that time, because of my ignorance. I could not understand why one would need to check several times if the door is locked, and still be so anxious about it.

Later when I started studying human behavioural sciences at a deeper level, I realized, it is a serious matter. In psychology, this behaviour is called Obsessive Compulsive Disorder or OCD. It is termed as a disorder between the brain and behaviour. The mind of a person suffering from OCD gets stuck on a particular thought or image that creates havoc in the mind. Actually, the obsession is the response to a feeling that may be deep rooted.

As PLR therapist, I come across many cases of OCDs where people are desperately looking for a solution, and the modality explains the phenomenon beautifully. They do understand the issue logically but are unable to help themselves; common OCDs are those involving a person constantly checking the door lock, gas knobs, taps, light switches, or reluctance to using public toilets, touch door knobs, shake hands; some people even wash their hands often, take frequent showers, hoard things or have intrusive thoughts.

When Rita came to meet me in my office, I noticed she was very fidgety and sat at the edge of her seat. She constantly felt the need to take showers. Since she was working, it was not possible for her to take a shower every time she felt she had to, but whenever she got an opportunity, she could not resist herself. The problem was that when she did not have a shower, she felt dirty and miserable and I realised that this was a case of OCD. Issues such as these are very sensitive in nature and need to be handled with care. Her close family was annoyed with Rita's habit and she understood everything logically but was helpless.

This was the first time I counselled a person with OCD. To start with, it was very important to calm her anxious nerves. The first step to solve any issue is to accept that there is an issue. Half the battle is won there. Rita was fighting too hard with her OCD. Through counselling, I was able to convince her that it is important to acknowledge the issue and it is possible to come out of it completely. She booked the next appointment for a PLR session.

The next time I saw Rita, there was already a positive change in her. The storm had calmed down. I could easily get her to relax and guide her to a past life memory where the root cause of her issue rested.

She went to a relevant past life where she saw herself as a beautiful girl in an Indian village. She was unmarried and studying in a college in a nearby village. One day while returning, some goons followed her, kidnapped and then gang raped her. After this incident, life was never the same for her. When the villagers learnt about the incident, they labelled her 'dirty' and ostracized her. She was asked to leave the village. She started to hate herself and eventually committed suicide. But the feeling that 'I have become dirty', stayed with her, and came back as an OCD in her current life.

During the session, at the deep theta level, I helped her embed the affirmation 'I love and accept myself, as I am' in her subconscious mind. Also, in the LBL state, her masters guided her to forgive the goons for their misdeeds.

It was difficult, but eventually we succeeded. With the help of higher understanding and forgiving, Rita's issue was completely resolved within a couple of weeks.

In another case, Delhi based Ajit had a unique issue too. He was extra cautious about anything related to fire. He would get very restless if somebody smoked in front of him and put the cigarette butt in an ashtray. He would check it several times. Ajit was also extra cautious about electric points and the switches. He would insist that his family wore slippers before touching any switch. He also obsessively checked the gas knobs at his home until he was totally convinced. These habits started interfering with his daily life, and left him miserable.

Ajit came to me with the hope of understanding the root cause of his issue and finding a solution. His keenness to find a solution and his readiness to undergo the therapy with an open and positive mind, made it a lot easier for me as a therapist.

The result was quite predictable. During the session, Ajit saw himself as a poor man working as an electrician in a city. One day, while on a job, there was a short circuit caused by his mistake, and the entire building caught fire. Before he could comprehend the situation, he was behind bars. He was petrified by this incident and eventually, died in the prison. The fear of something going wrong while dealing with any electrical or combustible material was a residue from the previous life in the form of an OCD, which subsided after a few sessions.

It has been observed that a deep-rooted, unexplainable fear is seated at the base of most OCDs. People suffering from it are labelled 'mentally ill'. But this is completely untrue. The theory of cause and effect says that one needs to reach the cause that is connected to the effect. Having an OCD is as normal as having ailments like diabetes or high blood pressure. Rather than hesitating to talk about it, one needs to accept and acknowledge it, and go to the root cause instead of just treating it symptomatically. It is generally related to an intense memory from a past life or sometimes even the past of the current life.

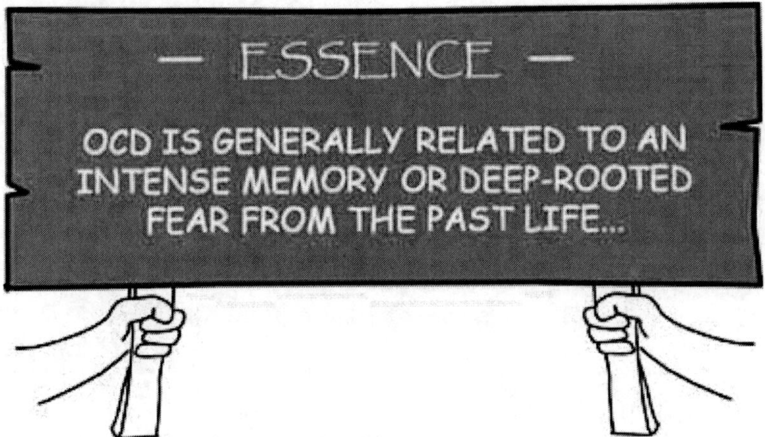

Reflections

10

WHY DO SOME PEOPLE HAVE BIRTH-MARKS OR BIRTH-DEFECTS?

IT SEEMS, HE WAS A
CASANOVA IN
PREVIOUS LIFE

10

On our soul journey,
from lifetime to lifetime

We carry our experiences,
and qualities sublime

Sometimes in the form of
emotions or birthmarks

All improving our experiences,
giving lessons prime

The past is gone, the future is yet to come and the present is what is. This is an unvarnished truth. However, the fact that all three are deeply interwoven cannot be overlooked. The memories of our past are indelibly imprinted on our body, mind and soul. These memories are carried forward in further incarnations, until they are completely resolved. One such roadmap to the memories of the past is the birth-marks or birth-defects.

Tracing birth-marks to past lives

The birth-marks usually travel to the next life, if there is an associated trauma with it that is not healed. It comes as a reminder either to heal or to learn a lesson that the wound is trying to teach. The darker the mark, the less the wound has healed karmicaly. The shape, size and colour can reveal a lot of things about the wound caused in the previous life and the extent of healing required. Birth-marks are caused by burns, wounds caused by bullets, arrows, or stabs, torture, or suicide. The cause and the solution can be easily found out by revisiting the previous life. Once the associated traumatic memory is released, and the lesson is learnt, the birth-mark fades away.

Reema, who was a participant in one of my workshops, came with the intention of finding the reason for an unusually large birth-mark on her left foot extending up to her thigh. This birth-mark was black when she was born, but slowly changed colour with age. Her mother had almost fainted when she saw this mark on baby Reema's leg. Along with the birth-mark, Reema, had one more issue. She was thirty-four and single. She had difficulties getting into a committed relationship. Her relationships, no matter who she dated, ended abruptly and on a sour note. During regression, Reema wanted to address these issues. She saw a relevant past life and when she shared the outcome, everyone in the workshop was dumbfounded.

Reema saw herself as a beautiful village girl in Gujarat, India in early 1900s. She lived with her parents and elder brother and she recalled her name as Kasturi. Her father earned his living through farming. They were poor, but happy. When Kasturi was 13 years old, she fell in love with the son of a wealthy zamindaar (landlord), whose name was Badal.

Both were madly in love. However, the community did not approve of this. Suddenly, the whole village turned against her. To escape from the ire of the villagers, her parents tried to marry her off, but Kasturi would create some scene and turn down the offer. The two had vowed to be together for the rest of their lives. The villagers came down on them like a ton of bricks. They threatened to kill her. It was difficult for both of them to live in the village in peace. They decided to elope. Badal's friends from the neighbouring village, offered to help them. Badal told Kasturi to stay put for a few days, until he went and made some arrangements in the neighbouring village. Kasturi had complete trust on the love of her life.

One day when the Badal was out of the village, about 20 villagers caught hold of her and dragged her to the farm. They threw her on a stack of hay and tied her hands and feet, so that she could not move. Her screams and pleads went unheard. Her parents just looked on helplessly. They had surrendered to the might of the villagers. The only person who could have rescued her from the miscreants was her boyfriend. He had promised to be there for her through every difficulty. But unfortunately he was out of the village.

After tying her to the stack of hay, one of the villagers lit the hay on fire. In a further ghastly act, one of them took a burning log of wood and rubbed it against her left leg. As the entire village witnessed this shameless act, the people who lead it announced, "If any of our village girls does what Kasturi did, she will have to face the same consequences." This whole act was aimed at creating terror amongst the villagers. Her body was charred. She was screaming and shouting in pain, but all of it fell on the deaf ears of the ruthless villagers. Her parents watched her die.

When Reema narrated her experience in the workshop, the other participants had tears in their eyes. Everyone was shocked when Reema showed us her left leg that had a dark red scar stretching from her foot up to her thigh. Another interesting thing happened during the session. When Kasturi's body was being burnt in that life, Reema's entire body was shaking during the session. Reema also mentioned that she was feeling the heat throughout her body. This was a somatic memory (memory being reproduced in a physical form) being released.

Nearly two years after this regression session, Reema came to my office to meet me. She looked very happy and peaceful. She had found the love of her life and was about to get married. Mysteriously, the scar on her left leg had faded considerably. Though this may sound like something out of a film with a happy ending, it was a scintillating real life experience.

Reliving the past life memories through birth-defects

A deformed body is a soul's way of remembering the memory of its cause, healing it and putting a closure. Some babies are born deformed. It may be in the form of missing limbs or have a club foot, bulging head, hunched back or a lump or deformity in some part of the body. Some people are born with a sensory or mental disability but each of these germinates in a past life.

This largely happens for two reasons. One, the soul has not had enough time between its incarnations to heal properly. Two, the mind needs to reconnect with the past life trauma so it can be healed and released. So a birth defect is formed at the site of the past life damage when the individual chooses to reincarnate into a new life. I would like to mention two distinct cases with physical disabilities. One of which was since birth while the other developed exactly at the same age of the death in the previous life.

Mitesh came to me with a defective and weak right hand. He told me that this condition was prevalent since his birth. He was a 25-year-old engineer, but still had great difficulty writing. He had to hold his right hand with his left hand even while writing his name. Thanks to the electronic age, he did not have to do much writing now but this disability bothered him and he was curious to learn the cause of it. During the conversation, I also noticed that he was depressed and subdued; while his friends were dating, and enjoying their lives, Mitesh avoided talking to girls and was an introvert.

We decided to go ahead with a past life regression session, mainly because this was greatly affecting his present life and he was desperate to find an answers to the many 'whys' in his life.

During the session he easily regressed into a relevant and immediate past life in a town in Madhya Pradesh, India in the 1940s. Coincidently, he was born in the same city in this life as well in 1980, though he no longer lives there.

Mitesh saw himself as a banker, from a middle-class family. He fell in love with a girl from a rich, orthodox and influential family. Given the time period, it was impossible for the girl's family to approve of this alliance, and so the couple decided to flee. Somehow, the family got a hint of this plan, and when the girl and boy tried to get out of town on his scooter, they were chased by a truck loaded with the girl's family's supporters. They stopped the two, sent the girl back home and brutally beat the boy. When the boy was lying in the middle of the road in a pool of blood, they drove the truck over his right hand, leaving him completely paralyzed.

After this incident, the boy spent a couple of years, bedridden and depressed. Later, he committed suicide.

This session was such a stark revelation of how the paralysed hand in the past life came as a birth defect in this lifetime. It also gave explanation for his depressive state of mind and his shying away from girls. He also identified that girl as one of his classmates in this lifetime. He had a crush on her since a young age but could never gather the guts to express his feelings.

The significant outcome of this session was that Mitesh felt more confident in life. Knowing the fact that this deformity had come from the past life, gave him some relief. It washed away the inferiority complex he had been carrying since his childhood, due of this defect. He was happier in life, having developed a higher understanding about why he had a defect.

It is possible to heal such birth-defects, though it may take a longer time and many sessions as the memory has manifested at the grossest level of our existence.

In yet another case, the deformity developed much later in life. However, it interestingly found its root into the past life.

Linda lives in Dallas, Texas. She was 35-year-old when she came to me for a session during her visit to India. She was anxious about a peculiar problem in her life which had suddenly propped up. Strangely, a lump appeared on her lower back out of nowhere. The diagnosis revealed that it was just a tissue formation and was not malignant. However, the course of medicines prescribed to her did not help. She came to me with a lot of hope.

During regression session, she went into a past life, where she saw herself as a female warrior in a Red Indian tribe and her head was shaven. Her name was Donoma. She was a skilled archer. There was always a rift going on between the neighbouring tribes. Once, such a neighbouring tribe attacked them. They reverted back with full force, but could not sustain for long. A point came, when they had to flee. Whoever was saved from the attack waded through the water to a boat which was anchored at the shore of a river on the outskirts of their village. As they rowed the boat towards another shore, the enemy's attack continued. Suddenly there was an explosion on the boat. Donoma along with her one year-old son tied to her back, jumped in the water and started swimming towards the shore. She was almost there, and as she was climbing the shore she felt a piercing pain in her back. Someone from the enemy camp had hit her with an arrow which pierced through her son to her back. She collapsed and finally died there. In the last moments, Donoma went through immense guilt that she could not save her son.

Linda developed a lump exactly at the same spot where the arrow had pierced her back at 35, the age at which she had died in the previous lifetime. During the session when she relived the memory, it was easy for her to release the guilt that was associated with the memory. After the session, Linda went back to Dallas. A couple of months later, I got a call from her informing that the lump on her back has dissolved completely.

When we come into greater awareness of our past lives, we understand that we are more than our current personality. We see that we are infinite beings and we connect with the truth about the totality of our existence. When we ask ourselves a question, 'who am I?', the answer leads us to learn more about our birth-marks and birth-defect s that are the roadmaps to our journey in past lives.

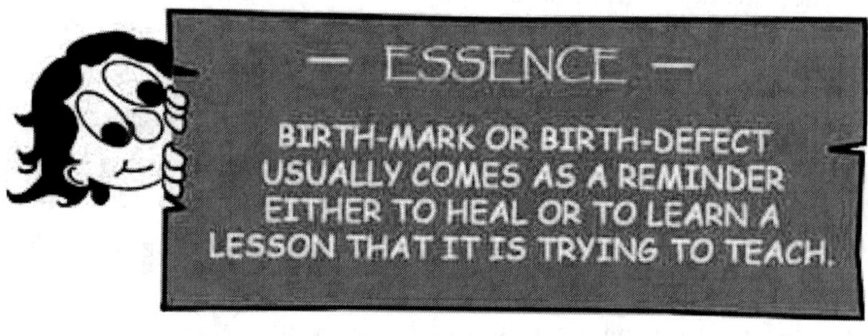

11

WHY DO SOME PEOPLE OR PLACES SEEM HAUNTINGLY FAMILIAR?

HISTORICAL
PALACE
KING XXX 1500 AD
WHOA...!!

11

I feel we've met, though
not sure when & where

It may just be fleeting, but
the feeling is true, I swear

Somewhere deep within,
I am sure and positive

You are someone close,
about whom I do care

Being a past life regression therapist, I am often asked, what real evidence is available to prove that we have lived before. My answer has always been the same – there are many! The most convincing evidence is the déjà vu experience. In fact, I would say that 50 per cent of my clients started believing in reincarnation because of a déjà vu experience.

Scientific explanations talk about how the experience is actually caused by a person having a brief glimpse of an object or situation, before the brain has completed constructing a full conscious perception of the experience. Such a 'partial perception' then results in a false sense of familiarity. Sure, that could be true for a few cases, but how does one explain déjà vu when a person visits a place so familiar they feel they've been there before. Some describe the experience as déjà visité.

I first visited South Africa in 1997 on a business trip. I went to visit the mines, as I was buying coal for a steel plant I was working for. As soon as the flight landed at Johannesburg International Airport (now called O. R. Tambo International Airport) and the door opened, the air seemed familiar. As I came out of the aircraft and went to my hotel, I got a very strong feeling that I have been here. The feeling was so surreal that I literally got goose-bumps but could not understand why I felt that way then.

The same evening, after checking into the hotel, I went out for a stroll. I didn't realize I was walking for about 45 minutes, and came so far that I could no longer remember which way I came from. I kept walking and something told me that if I turn to my left, I would reach St. John's College and chapel. I took a few steps to my left and there the huge old building was. This was my first visit to the city; so obviously, I was surprised but knew this wasn't just a coincidence. During that walk, I also knew how to get to the spice market, Rissik Street Post Office and an old worn-out garage. It was like I knew the streets of the city very well. Somehow, I also seemed to understand and pick up the local Zulu and Afrikaans languages easily.

Now you may think that sometimes it is the intuition that can guide you. Absolutely right. But the difference is, déjà vu is when you feel 'I have been here before', whereas psychic intuition will only give you information about a particular thing. The knowing that 'I was here' cannot come by intuition; rather it is a deeper inner feeling, which cannot be explained in words. In my case, I even confirmed having lived in Johannesburg in my immediate previous life through a past life regression session. That's the best part of this therapy; whatever we suspect can be validated and confirmed.

During my session, I saw myself as a black coal miner in South Africa, somewhere around the year 1910. I stayed in the ghetto in the southern part of Johannesburg, along with my wife and kids. I saw myself living in extremely poor circumstances. The apartheid was at its peak, and whites had complete political control over all other racial groups. The law prevented black mine workers from practicing skilled trades. I was against this and wanted to fight. I saw myself joining a movement started by Mahatma Gandhi in 1915 (by that time, he had already returned to India). Since the movement was against the government, fellow coal miners, who also joined the movement, and I were put behind bars. I lost my job and was in complete penury. I saw myself dying at the age of around 71, surrounded by my family. While dying, I had the regret that I could not look after my family well.

In the same lifetime, I also saw myself going through an almost fatal drowning experience inside a coal mine, details of which I have mentioned in the chapter of fears and phobias. Like me, there are many people who experience the similar phenomenon of déjà vu.

Hardeep once talked about his first trip to a gurudwara on the outskirts of Patiala, Punjab. He was only about four years old when his parents took him there and as soon as he entered the premises, he ran inside, found a large portrait of a granthi (priest), in the passage and stood starring at it. When his parents asked him what happened, Hardeep said that it was his picture. The parents tried to explain that it was not possible, but he disagreed. Hardeep told them about how he sat in the gurudwara and sang devotional songs. By then, a few visitors and gurudwara helpers gathered around and started asking questions to the boy. Surprisingly, he had all the answers. He knew exactly how the granthi died, which was while tying a flag to a tall pole. He even led everyone to a room that the granthi lived in. This room had been locked for many years. Without even entering it, my friend described the contents of a box owned by the granthi. The gurudwara staff later checked and confirmed the contents, just as he described. Hardeep later met the granthi's sons, who had grown up and his wife who was old. They could not believe what they saw and heard. Even today, Hardeep remembers everything and has taken his present life wife to the same gurudwara. He says, these memories do not affect him in his present life, as he has a higher understanding that they belong to the past and have no relevance to the present.

How can these experiences be logically explained?

We store our memories (of the present life and past lives) deep in the subconscious mind. These memories travel along with our soul from body to body. So, when we see a place in a present life that we have been to in a previous life, a memory from that life activates itself and we have a deep inner knowledge or feeling that we've been there before. Déjà vu also happens when you meet people. Have you heard people asking, "Have we met before?" even when they are meeting you for the first time. Sometimes certain sounds or certain tastes or smells seem familiar, although we have never encountered those before.

These are nothing but past life memories revisited. This can be triggered by any of our senses. In other words, these memories come to our conscious awareness through the sense of sight if the person is visual, or through sound, taste or smell, depending on which of our sense organs is dominant. Sometimes it can just be a deep inner knowing that guides us. Since I am a visual person, the whole picture was in front of me, with the directions when I was in Johannesburg.

The experience of déjà vu can sometimes be inconceivable

Mita, who came to me for a session, narrated an experience. She visited Konark temple in Orrisa, with a group of friends, a few years back. She was too excited to be there and was moving around oblivious of her friends and other people. She took her friends to the ruins behind the temple. There, they saw was an old courtyard in front of a stone platform. Mita said she used to dance in the courtyard, and the king would sit on the platform. There was an area behind the temple that was barricaded. Mita felt a strong urge to go there. She told her friends that there was an old Shiva temple there, where she would go to pray, every day before she performed. Her friends were utterly confused by her words. Mita insisted that she visits that temple. They had to try really hard to take necessary permissions to venture into the barricaded area. To everyone's surprise, there was a Shiva temple there, exactly as Mita had described.

This is unbelievable but true. Such experiences can be validated by visiting that particular life. It is also possible to find out how some people are related to us. At times, we experience love or hate at first sight. This generally happens at the time of finding one's life partner. We feel that we know the other person so well and are meant to be together for the rest of our lives. Often, we meet somebody accidently for the first time yet the person's face seems familiar. Later, we may develop a strong bond with that person, which may be thicker than blood relations.

Sometimes déjà vu experiences can be confusing and interfere with the current life. I know of a girl, who was happily married with a daughter and was pursuing her career. Everything was going well in her life until she switched her job. There she met a man, who she felt, she knew since ages. One day, she got a dream where she saw that this man was her lover in the past birth. Coincidently, the boy, who was also married, shared the same feelings. It was a shocking coincidence, but they started developing an affinity towards each other. This started affecting their present marital relationships. A past life regression session helped both of them to understand this attraction. They also got a message from their master in the LBL state to let go of each other and focus on their current life and partners. This wisdom helped them resolve their mental mess.

Sometimes, situations and people may seem hauntingly familiar and create chaos in our minds. This confusion disappears when we develop greater consciousness and higher understanding. Similarly, there is no reason to fret when some children talk about something unusual and as parents, we need to understand that there is some memory waiting to be released. The sooner the memory is resolved, the better it is for the child as this will eliminate the potential threat of meddling with the current life.

My friend once described a peculiar memory of her early life. When she was three-year-old, and had just started speaking, she used to describe the interiors of an aircraft in detail. The fact was that she had never travelled in an aircraft before. Along with this she also used to see herself lying in a pool of blood. When she spoke about this for the first time, her mom was scared and tried discourage her from talking about this. This slowly reduced as she grew up, but the curiosity of what it was, remained. She felt that something was unresolved within her and this did bother her sometimes. We decided to do a regression session to find out the cause.

During regression she went into an immediate past life, where she saw herself as a wealthy business woman based in London. She owned a private aircraft and travelled to various countries for business purpose. On one such trip when she was coming back from Paris to London, in her private jet along with her four male colleagues, the tragedy happened. As the aircraft was about to land at the London airport, it hit a tree and crashed.

The next thing she saw was that she was lying in a pool of blood and some people were taking to the hospital – the vision she used to see as a child. In the hospital when she was operated upon she could hear doctors telling her that she will be fine. When I asked her to move forward during regression and go to the next day, she told me that there was no next day. She had left her body in that life. Coincidently she could remember the name of the aircraft and the month and year of crash. We checked the details on the internet and the facts were actually validated.

After the session, she experienced inner peace and felt that the puzzle in her life was solved. Whatever we feel is rooted somewhere within our past and those feelings should never be disowned as they are a part of our personality. It is our responsibility to address and resolve them.

Child prodigies – The reincarnated geniuses

We often hear about child prodigies – children with extraordinary capabilities and talents. In psychology research literature, the term child prodigy is defined as a person under the age of ten who produces meaningful output in some domain to the level of an adult expert performer. They can be called reincarnated geniuses.

How else can you explain the amount of knowledge and ability that these people have at such a young age? Mozart, for example, was composing music by the age of five. Even if you started teaching a normal child music by the age of two or three, how many would be composing by five, or even master their instruments? Prodigies retain knowledge of a past life or lives; maybe not consciously, because they normally undergo some kind of rudimentary training. But they seem to grasp the lessons easily and quickly surpass the teacher.

If you spend a lifetime learning a particular skill or profession, and then are reborn with residual knowledge of all that you learned, you would be a prodigy in that field. When children with such abilities are suppressed and not given proper space to thrive and grow, they often end up depressed. We are souls on individual journeys, but at the same time we also have the prime responsibility to help each other grow and evolve in this journey.

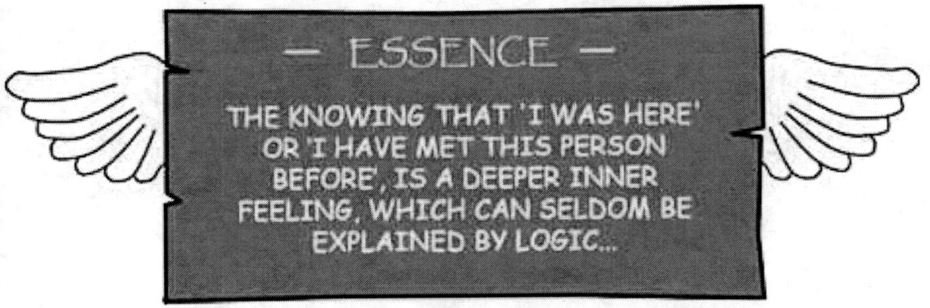

Reflections

12

WHAT IS THE PURPOSE OF MY LIFE?

$e=mc^2$
HE SAYS, HIS PURPOSE IS TO TEACH...

12

Before I was born,
I knew about my journey

The purpose I chose,
that will set me free

With the guidance of master,
I set forth on the path

Going deeper and exploring,
gives me the key

"I know I am supposed to be doing something else, but don't know what."

I am sure this thought must have crossed your mind at least once. A thought like this often gets overshadowed by everything else around us. As soon as it comes, paying bills and doing the routine chores suddenly gain higher priority. Soon, we get convinced that such thoughts are impractical and easily dismiss them. We all have unrealized dreams and undeveloped talents deep within us. Probably a clue to 'what I want to do' lies there. Every instance in our life slowly takes us closer to that calling. Something that generates restlessness, irritation or frustration or something that attracts, motivates or inspires offer indications. All of these lead to the surfacing of inner calling – the purpose of our life. It could be found through the obstacles, problems, or through something that we may admire in someone. It may also be seen in those abilities in us we may not think are special, but are appreciated by others.

It is said that, when we as souls manifest in the physical form, we come with the knowing of our purpose. We remember that purpose as well as the events we planned in the spirit world to lead us there, till the tender age of about three. Thereafter this knowing gets buried beneath the layers of conditioning as we grow up. We get influenced by people around us and thus start living a life of their choice. For example, my chosen purpose could be excelling an art. But people around me including my parents may feel that 'arts cannot be pursued as a profession, one needs a job for livelihood'. Getting influenced by their opinions, I may stop following my inner calling, and finally get into the pattern of life others decide for me.

For some, a life's purpose could be earning money, while for some, it could be serving others, or excelling in sports or mastering an art, or learning a virtue like forgiveness, gratitude, or dealing with an emotion. A purpose that has been consciously forgotten can also be revealed in deep mediation or during a moment of transcendence such as a near death experience (NDE) or during a past life regression session.

Once 28-year-old Riny Sengupta, came to me referred by a

friend, who read my article in a local newspaper. The article was about past life regression and there was a mention of how I found my life's purpose through this therapy. After doing her master's degree, Riny had a lucrative job in an insurance company. She had a perfect life but felt a void within. She fixed up an appointment with me for the session. She had come with an open mind and wanted to find her purpose if possible.

During the session, Riny saw a life when she was a Buddhist monk in the north-eastern part of India, teaching other monks. She saw her complete life as a monk, who died in a peaceful and happy state. In the LBL state, she saw herself teaching underprivileged children. There was a knowing that what she is being shown is her purpose in this lifetime.

A few days after the regression, she chose to leave her highly paid job and joined an NGO as a volunteer and was involved in teaching underprivileged children. She just wanted to follow her purpose. Riny is now working for a leading philanthropic organisation, impacting the education space through a leadership program for teachers. When I met Riny after a few months of the session, the glow on her face and her beaming smile said it all.

Following your purpose fills you with the energy that makes your life worthwhile and fulfilling. It fills you with inner peace and happiness.

In another case, Dipti Gandhi, who runs an NGO for children with special needs, attended one of my workshops. She belongs to an affluent family, and given her situation, anyone would just enjoy life and make merry. But somehow, she was pulled to serve these children. Looking at her passion and dedication for this cause people often asked her if she had a special child or what motivated her to work so passionately for this cause. A volunteer once offered to work for her organization and as time passed, Dipti got attached to her emotionally, which was very unlikely for her nature. She was very uncomfortable with this and wanted to know why she felt this attachment to an outsider.

During the session of finding the purpose of life in my workshop, she went into a life where she saw herself as the mother of a special child. She saw that due to societal pressure, she abandoned that child later. She felt guilty when she realized her mistake. But she had already taken a step that could not be reversed. So to settle the karmas and learn the virtues of compassion, love and patience, she chose this as her purpose in this lifetime. She realized that the abandoned child of her past life was none other than the volunteer whom she was emotionally attached to.

Following our purpose, invariably gives us an inner satisfaction and a sense of fulfilment. Every soul on its journey is slowly moving towards his or her purpose, knowingly or unknowingly.

It's almost like we are all being pulled towards our purpose with an invisible string. However, if we are conscious about it, we can take concrete steps towards it in this lifetime.

It is very interesting to note that when we align ourselves to our purpose of life, we create a magnetic field around us by which we attract people, events and opportunities in our life. These in turn help us move towards the purpose. This magnetic field is often governed by our beliefs, attitude, past experiences, unresolved emotions, expectations, and more. However, the magnetic field loses its power through our thoughts, language and action of fear, resentments, self-criticism, negative beliefs, taking revenge, blaming others for our situation and so on. On the other hand the magnetic field gains its power through gratitude, faith, trust, courage, forgiveness and love.

I know of a couple that has a special child. Both are highly talented, Indian classical singers and are very passionate about singing. They are battling hard to attain monetary stability. But when they perform, they not only lose the track of time but also completely loose themselves in the music. In spite of all the difficulties they face each day, I have never seen them getting angry on the child or letting it affect their passion. The kind of unconditional love and affection they both are giving to the child is remarkable.

In my past life regression workshops, one of the sessions is 'Meeting your Master', where we come face to face with our master or guardian angel, who has been guiding us through many life times. During this meditative process, the master may appear in front of us in the form known to us or just as a ball of light. We can see or feel the presence of the masters during meditation, and can communicate with them through our thoughts. It is quite a surreal experience. Along with our purpose of life, we can get many questions about our life answered.

One of my workshop participants, Kanika Bahl wrote to me about a beautiful experience, through an email. She had an insightful experience during the workshop. I do not wish to pollute it by editing; hence I'm reproducing it as it is with Kanika's consent.

Let me begin with a big thank-you to Santosh. The profound experience I had after meeting my master was more than dreams come true.

On the count of 10-1, I opened the door and saw my master sitting on a black flattened stone The cave was dark. He looked not more than 17 years old with a very thin face enveloped with a trimmed beard and shoulder length hair. What followed next was a 'Rapid fire round'. I would prefer to pen down that as dialogues as that is how I experienced, referring him as 'MB' and myself as 'K'

K: Who are you? I have never seen you before.

MB: I am Mahavtar Baba.

K: What? Mahavtar Baba !! But you are alive and live in the Himalayas.

MB: Yes.

K: Then can I see you in real.

MB: You are seeing me.

K: Is this really happening or am I just imagining.

MB: This is happening.

K: Babaji, what is the purpose of my life?

MB: What you are doing right now is your purpose.

K: You mean courtyard is my purpose?

(The courtyard is my day-care and preschool for children 6 months to 6 years)

MB : Yes and you are their 'Spiritual Mother'.

K: What did you just say... spiritual mother !

MB: Yes spiritual mother.

After this I started crying and could not believe as if it was all happening for real.

K: Spiritual mother , thank you so much, but you think I am worthy and capable of being so? I mean this is a huge responsibility.

MB: Yes, I prepared you for this and now I will work through you, you are my instrument . After 2005 very high souls have come on this earth and I want you to take care of them as their spiritual mother along with their biological mother. They will come to you from 6 months to 6 years of age.

I can correlate now why he said "I prepared you". It's been a long journey in this birth and God consciousness has been very predominant in my life for past 20 years.

K: Babaji, I have 27 children and it is a fact when I go there I just love being with them and I feel so much at home and I pour out lot of motherly love.

MB: You will go up to 56 and all the resources will be provided to you.

K: Will I be able to open more such centres?

MB: You are limitless.

K: What about my partner Bela . How did she and I come together and now we get along as if we were always together.

Babaji immediately took me to the past life where Bela and I were together. It was a beautiful gurukul. I saw her from a distance teaching 8-9 year old kids. I was sitting with little girls and doing some craft and needlework.

It is a fact that ever since my partner and me started our preschool and day-care , we have felt a very strong divine presence guiding us for everything . With the least of efforts all resources have fallen into our laps before we needed them. As if all this was always meant to be.

K: Babaji you come and bless my school.

In a split second we were standing in the courtyard. He said it is already blessed and turned round 3-4 times. I could see some of the children playing around. Then we came back to the cave.

By then the buzzer went off and Santosh told us to leave the cave and come back.

K: Babaji can I touch your feet.

Babaji allowed me to touch his feet.

I told Babaji I want to know more. He said, "It will be revealed to you". He showed me his left hand and gave the gesture to move back.

I came out of the cave and was back into the conscious world !

Warm regards,

Kanika .

This is how we are actually able to communicate with our master, in the meditative state. Kanika was happy at the reassurance from her master about her purpose of life that she was already following.

SELFIE WITH THE MASTER ...

As described earlier our purpose may be revealed to us through our special abilities or through something that people appreciate of us. Nevertheless whatever the purpose may be, the path towards our purpose is always a bumpy ride. There comes a point many times when we may feel like giving it all up. It requires endurance, commitment, dedication, strength and courage to follow it. When my friend Anju Musafir and her husband Pascal Chazot decided to follow their purpose, the hurdles they faced were immense. But they put up a brave front at every challenge that came their way. It is an inspiring story in Anju's own words.

My husband Pascal completed his post as a director in 1996, of the Alliance Francaise d'Ahmedabad, a learning centre that offered French classes. He introduced some innovative language learning/teaching techniques there. The centre became so popular that some parents of the students, wished their children could enjoy learning at their respective schools as much as they enjoyed learning French.

Pascal and I had a vision. We wanted to create an international school where children are happy and the learning is meaningful and enjoyable. We wanted to create a school where quality education is accessible to all sections of society. Pascal proposed that the school offers free education to 20% municipal school children. It should be free for the poor, and those who can afford should pay. It will cross-subsidise. As we began exploring this thought, we realized how difficult it was to change the existing systems. Authorities had to be convinced, permissions and sanctions had to be taken, huge amount of funds were required; all these were few of the primary challenges. Pascal has taken leave without pay from his secure Government job in France, to accomplish this. As time passed, we ran out of resources. The struggle was on going. Exasperated, one day I asked Pascal, "How will we succeed without any resources?" Calmly, he answered, "If our intention is pure, the means will come." Not too convinced by the reply, I turned away, shaking my head and was dumbstruck at what I saw. There was a hoarding with Mahatma Gandhi's message, 'Find the purpose, the means will follow.' It was probably nature's way of stamping our decision. From that day on, this applied in everything we did. We were guided and provided.

Convinced by our idea and seeing our resolve, the then Ahmedabad Municipal Commissioner asked us to meet him with the project proposal. He was kind enough to allocate a building for this after some legal formalities. The AMC created a trust and incorporated us as trustees.

Happy with first step, we were only naïve to think that it was a smooth road ahead. There were lobbies protesting against the project. An entire agitation started: there were people on the streets, buses were burnt, 'jail-bharo-andolan' started, placards of 'Simon go back', blood signature campaigns, stoning of public property, violence, relay fasts etc. There were different lobbies: some against the idea of English as a medium language, some against the international schools, some against the idea of a mixed population comprising different religions, castes and the economic backgrounds. But all together were against the idea of a foreigner on the board of trustees. They saw Pascal's inclusion as a trustee under the lens of a colonial legacy and imperialism. The agitations spread from city to city under political patronage of certain groups and misguided perceptions. It reached even the national capital and made daily headlines in local papers.

Pascal decided to fast unto death for his ideals, but was dissuaded by concerned citizens of the city who warned that he could be used as a political pawn, which could diminish the cause.

Every night, I would go to bed crying unable to take this. We were surrounded several times by angry mobs hurling obscenities at us, and attacking us. Unable to see my distress Pascal decided to leave the project. However, one morning when I woke up, I wondered 'how can I give up without trying? I must give it the best fight I can'. That was the least I could do. I decided to become Pascal's strength.

Universe tests your resolve at every step. Once I decided to do this there were some divine souls who understood our Gandhian philosophy and thought in creating a democratic school based on non-violence, and stood by us. This was followed by a PIL filed by an agitating group in High court and the school building was sealed. The case then went to the supreme court. Some renowned lawyers came forth and fought the case on our behalf benevolently.

At that time, as a stop-gap measure, we were running KG classes with 18 children in a small bungalow. When I announced that we won the case and we could go to our own building, little 4 year old Kartiki looked at me and said in Hindi "Acche logo ki hamesha jeet hoti hain na?" (Good people always win don't they?). My eyes welled up with tears.

Thus Mahatma Gandhi International School was born; a school where there are no text-books, rigid time-tables, marks, school bells, uniforms and board exams. We brought in a project based inter-disciplinary learning that had links to children's real life and context, where learning and evaluation were stress free. The Right to Education Act 2010 incorporates all these facets. For a small school, we succeeded in creating a space for an alternative to the 'prison' and 'factory model' of education as described by French philosopher Michel Foucault.

Paradoxically, the people who protested came to us for the admission of their children. We named our school after Mahatma Gandhi as his words became our mantra, 'Find the purpose, the means will follow'.

The greatest spiritual truth is that we are one with our creator. Hence our individual purpose is intertwined with the universal purpose. Finding and following our purpose takes us a step higher in the process of evolution. If we look at life in the light of 'whatever happens or doesn't happen with us is taking us towards our purpose', we are able to see various hidden aspects of life, which we are otherwise oblivious of. By doing so, each moment becomes a creative opportunity to develop ourselves. If we are able to expand this understanding, we experience an internal energy shift or shift of consciousness, ultimately leading to our purpose. The role of the universe is to help us reach where we are supposed to. It helps us by giving signals from time to time. Success depends on how well we are able to interpret and follow these.

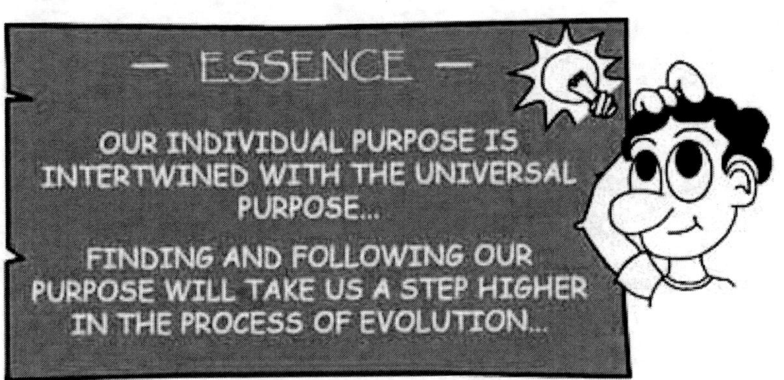

Reflections

13

SECRETS OF THE SOUL

NOW
WHAT ??
JUST HAVE FAITH IN
'LAW OF
REINCARNATION' ...

13

We are spirit beings,
experiencing human life
Growing in the process,
through problems and strife,
Our soul is divine,
part of that great source
Evolving and learning,
life after life

Most of us have experienced moments when some incidents such as near fatal accidents, death of loved ones, or even a tragedy read in the news papers, have suddenly centred our focus on the fundamental questions of our existence. Why am I here?, where do I come from?, where do I go?, what happens after death?, and who am I?, are few of such questions that make us turn inwards and reflect. If we don't try to go deeper at that time, they are lost and forgotten in the chaos of our lives. It is necessary to delve in to these questions, to understand the purpose of life, its deeper meaning and to raise our consciousness. Once we understand the process, our perspective of looking at everything in life changes significantly.

Who am I?

This is one of the most vital questions I am often asked.

During my workshops I do a small exercise, with a volunteer from amongst the participants. In one such workshop, the volunteer was Raj.

My first question to Raj was, "Who are you?"

He replied, "My name is Raj. I am 6' tall. I am 30 years old. I have a healthy body and a fair complexion. I am an engineer by profession."

"Fair enough, that's your physical description. Now tell me, who are you?"

Raj said, "I am generally energetic but at times have my low phases when I feel completely drained. I have a lot of physical and mental energy to sustain all odds, but emotionally I break down at times."

"Aren't you now describing your energy states Raj? Is that you?"

"Well, I am an emotional person. I am short-tempered, but I am very loving and friendly by nature."

"You are talking about your emotions, Raj. Tell me, who are you?"

This really got Raj thinking. After a pause, he said, "Well I am an intellectual person. I am very clear about my likes and dislikes. I believe in making the right choice and I take time to arrive at any decision."

"What you just described is your mental or intellectual makeup. But you have still not answered my question; who are you?"

Now Raj got confused, but he was not going to give up easily. The other participants were intensely listening to this conversation, mentally answering the questions. Everyone was eager to know what this was leading to.

After a long pause, Raj said, "Maybe, I am all of these combined."

"All right, now I want you to drop all these four descriptions of yourself and tell me, who are you?"

"If I drop all these, I experience bliss, happiness and peace," pat came the reply. I was happy that we were almost there. There was peace on Raj's face. Since every participant was doing this exercise mentally, peace radiated in the entire room.

"Okay, now, for one last time, just try to think – who are you? Are you the bliss, happiness or peace?"

There was absolute silence in the room. I could see all the participants deeply absorbed in themselves searching for the answer to the question 'who are you?' That was the whole intention of this exercise. To make people dive deep down into their consciousness.

With a winning smile on his face, as if he found a long lost treasure, Raj replied, "I cannot be bliss, happiness or peace, I am experiencing all these, so 'I' have to be the one who is experiencing, observing or witnessing all of this. So I am none of these."

Raj arrived there and so did the other participants. We had just touched that inner core, that self or the soul, which is covered by these five bodies.

What is a soul?

The soul is the self, the "I" that inhabits the body and acts through it. It is the part of that great divine source, which goes through the process of evolution to develop itself. The soul consists of two parts – *jiva* and *aatma*. *Jiva* is the outer covering, which carries memories, emotions, experiences and karmas. The inner part of the soul is *aatma*, which is a part of the Source and goes through the process of evolution, life after life. As we evolve, *aatma* expands, and the outer cover *jiva* shrinks until at a certain point, *jiva* becomes null. This happens when the memories, emotions, experiences and karmas completely dissolve. This is the point of enlightenment, *nirvana* or self-realization; when we become pure consciousness again; ready to mix back with the Source.

On the gross level, we as human beings in the physical body, experience this physical world through our five senses, namely touch, smell, sight, taste and hearing. Whereas soul experiences this world through its five senses, which are love, empathy, trust, peace and intuition. These are called the language of soul and is largely based on feelings. The soul goes through various lifetimes adopting different bodies, but carries with it the unresolved memories and the karmas from previous lifetimes. The soul is immortal, living in a mortal body.

What happens after death?

DEATH, as I put it, is a Doorway to our Eternal And True Home. We, as souls, come to the earth plane and house ourselves in a physical body to learn and evolve spiritually. Hence, earth is considered to be a school and a temporary accommodation, during our long journey of many lifetimes.

People who have undergone Near Death Experiences (NDE), have reported having seen a tunnel of light or tunnel of darkness and reaching the life between life space. This state (LBL) is where we spend time after our death or before we go into a new life. Here we meet our masters and guiding angles and other souls who have passed away before us. With the help of our master, we review the life just spent and assess our progress. Since we go through lot of challenges during our life on earth, we need to take rest, so that we are energized and ready to reincarnate. During the LBL state, we are in the company of angles, who shower unconditional love upon us. Once we are ready to take a new life, we plan our next life, its purpose and challenges, the people we are going to be associated with, our parents, our place of birth, etc. with the help and guidance of our master. Thus we are ready to be born again.

The time we spend in the LBL state depends on the weight of our karmas, which is governed by 'karmic gravity'. Heavy or negative karmas increase our pull towards the earth plane, due to karmic gravity, and bring us back on earth from the LBL state. However light or positive karmas allow us to spend more time in the LBL state.

Thus this cycle of life and death continues, until we evolve to a stage where our karmic balance becomes nil and we do not need to take birth again. This is the culmination of the long journey of evolution. This is the point of *nirvana,* after which if we take birth, it is only for helping other souls to uplift themselves on the path of evolution.

As long as we identify ourselves with the body, we are living within the boundaries of time and possibilities. However the "I" that we truly are, is pure consciousness that is timeless and limitless.

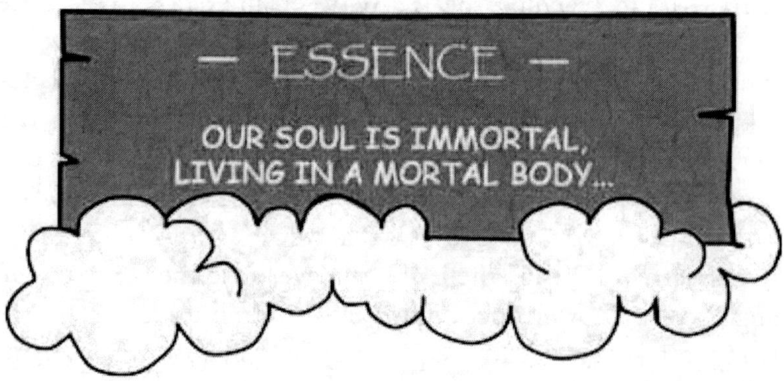

14

WHAT IS PAST LIFE REGRESSION?

HOW DID THE
SESSION GO DEAR...?
DID YOU SEE YOUR
PAST...?

14

I can heal myself,
by reliving the past
By releasing my emotions,
traumas no longer last
Reliving is relieving,
is a strong mantra
By going through the process,
our future's die is cast.

Past life regression is a process through which one can revisit the memories of previous lives, with an intention of resolving or releasing them. It is based on the premise that whatever we are today, our identity as a person is the result of our past – the past of this life as well as the past of previous lives. Our past thus dictates our present and thereby shapes our future. Therefore it implies that if we are facing any issue in the present, the root cause of that issue can be traced back in the past. These issues if not resolved over time can mess up our present and our future. Past life regression is one such tool that can help us reach the root cause and resolve it there. By doing so, we are able to put a closure to those trouble causing memories and issues and subsequently loosen their hold over our current life situations.

Storage and retrieval of memories

To understand the past life memories, let us take a sneak-peek into our mind. Our mind is one magical computer. It has two parts – the conscious mind and subconscious mind. Our conscious mind is like the tip of the iceberg constituting only 4% of the total mind, whereas our subconscious mind is 96%. The subconscious mind is a storehouse of memories, potential and wisdom. Without consciously being aware of it, each and every incident, small or big, gets automatically recorded in our subconscious mind as a memory. Along with the memory, the emotions we experience at that moment also get attached with that memory. Any memory by itself is neutral and does not have an impact on us. But the attached emotion can have a great influence on our life. For instance, let's say, a boss fires an employee in the office. This incident is recorded in the employee's mind as a memory. Along with the memory, whatever emotions the employee goes through at that moment (such as anger or frustration), also gets attached to the memory and gets stored in the subconscious mind as suppressed emotions. These emotions ultimately become the root cause of employee's behavioural pattern, personality traits, reactions, or circumstance in his present life.

We experience several such emotions every day. This process is not only taking place since the time we are in our mother's womb in this lifetime, but also through all our previous lifetimes. If these suppressed emotions are not released, they start interfering in our present life. They influence our reactions, the decisions we take, our choices, relationships and practically everything in our life along with our physical and emotional wellbeing.

Whatever we are today is the result of our past. These suppressed negative emotions that are the root cause of issues in the present life need to be released from our subconscious mind. This can be done through regression. Reliving is relieving. This means that if a memory is relived as if it is happening now, it comes to our conscious awareness and is released. This can be compared with a can filled with air, when taken deep inside a pool and opened, air bubbles get released, and they come on the surface and disappear. By releasing, we are relieved from the traumas or effects of that memory and emotion. By offloading the past baggage, our future journey becomes easier.

The various states of mind

Mapping our brain activity through an EEG, will show that in a day, we surf through various levels of the mind. Brain activity can be measured in terms of cycles per second (cps).

When brain activity is above 40 cps, which is the gama level, it is an anxious state of mind. When our mind is busy thinking, engaged in work and alert, where brain activity is 13-40 cps, it's the beta state of mind. Next is the alpha state of mind operating at 8-13 cps, which is a relaxed, self-introspective and meditative state. The next level is the theta state of mind where brain activity is 4-7 cps. This state is the deep meditative state. While sleeping, this is where our dreams come from. It is also the state where our memories are stored. The last one is the delta state, which is a deep sleep and a dreamless state measuring 1-4 cps.

Our past life memories are also stored in the theta level of mind. These memories are stored in the form of thoughts, images, sounds, taste, smells or somatics and are reproduced in the same way.

Process of past life regression

The path to the subconscious mind is through progressively relaxing the body and then the mind. This state can also be achieved through hypnosis. A past life regression therapist is essentially a facilitator, who helps the subject reach deeper levels of the subconscious mind and release the memories and suppressed emotions of relevant past lives. This results in healing of issues and traumas of the present life. After landing in a particular life, the therapist helps the subject go back and forth in that lifetime to experience significant events. These memories can be experienced by the subject in the form of vivid visuals, feelings or thoughts. The therapist also takes the subject to the moment of death in that life and then into the LBL state. During this state, the subject reviews the entire life experienced, the repetitive patterns in that life, and the lessons therein, with help of the master. Once this is done, the subject is slowly brought back to present consciousness. The whole process takes about two to three hours.

Who can undergo past life regression?

If one experiences any of the following, one can go for a past life regression therapy. PLRT is considered as an effective alternate therapy and resolves the issues from its roots. This also helps in balancing the karmas and acts as a booster to one's spiritual journey.

- Inexplicable health problems that do not respond to conventional therapies, such as phantom pains, asthma, skin issues, etc.
- Irrational fears and phobias, such as claustrophobia, hydrophobia, acrophobia, etc.

- Emotional traumas like anger, depression, low self-esteem, etc.
- Relationship issues which may be between parent-child, with in-laws, business acquaintances, etc.
- Repetitive patterns in life, in which one gets stuck
- A desire to know the purpose of life
- Stagnation on the spiritual path
- Curiosity about past lives.

Common misconceptions about PLRT

During my workshops or the discussions on PLRT, I face a lot of questions from curious seekers. It is natural to have questions and doubts regarding this topic of death and life after death, as it tends to be guarded as a deeper secret. I have put down some of the doubts that people share with me, which I am sure must have occurred to you as well.

<u>Only the present life is relevant and past lives are not</u>

I believe that one should always live in the present moment. At the same time, however, if there is something from the past that pulls us back, it is important to resolve it completely. Only then we are able to live fully in the present moment and tap our highest potential.

<u>It is not possible to see past lives, it is just a made up story</u>

The process of regression is such that while going to the deeper states of the mind, our logical or conscious mind goes in the sleep mode. In a deep state of trance, we are experiencing everything from our subconscious. Imagination is a part of our conscious mind, and hence whatever we experience while in trance has to be a memory coming out.

The past life memories experienced during regression are due to suggestions of the therapist

The therapist's job is to make you land in the past life. Thereafter the memories that pop out are a very personal experience. The therapist's job is reduced to simply help you sail through that life and bring you back to the present moment.

One loses control of self, once in trance and one might get stuck in the past life

On the contrary one is in complete control of oneself as the awareness expands. If at any given time one feels uncomfortable, one has to just open the eyes to come back to the present moment. It is impossible to get stuck in a past life, as it is only a memory that one is experiencing.

One might feel disoriented after regression, affecting the present life

One can feel disoriented, but for a very short period of time. It can be compared to the feeling of waking up from a deep sleep. It does not affect the present life and the issue is resolved and healed. Moreover one develops a higher understanding about life and its issues. It is spiritual process and is absolutely safe.

Past life regression has numerous benefits and is the only therapy that allows us to go back in time to correct the things that were not right. It helps us experience the non-physical dimensions and access the universal knowledge and the divine plan. Once in that realm, one can move back and forth without the restraint of space and time. Such experiences can bring about profound transformations. Past life regression is not only an amazing healing tool, but also helps us find answers to the most intriguing questions about ourselves and the universe. It relieves us from the biggest fear a human being has – the fear of death. Experiencing past lives helps us broaden our perspective and thus come out of the narrow, restrictive thinking, understanding the bigger picture of life.

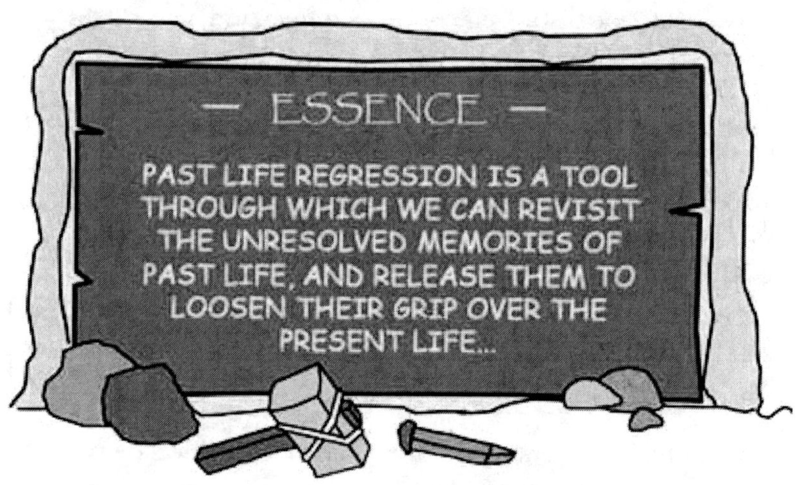

15

WHERE ARE YOU ON THE JOURNEY OF EVOLUTION?

THIS WAY
ENLIGHTENMENT
I WONDER, HOW FAR I'VE REACHED...

15

I wish I know
where am I,
On my soul journey
before I die,
So that I can
make corrections,
By knowing Universal laws
that I can apply...

We all are on a spiritual expedition. As we incarnate from lifetime to lifetime, we learn lessons, gather experiences and fulfil soul agreements. Each one of us is on an individual soul journey. Our paths and purpose may be different but our destination is one. On the way, we meet several other souls who may be at different levels of evolution. If we are able to get clarity about our current location on the map of this journey, we can move ahead with greater awareness about the process.

As discussed in chapter of disparity, we go through seven stages of evolution from Infant soul to Infinite soul. It is a long journey and we spend several lifetimes in various stages. We are responsible only for our own evolution, and hence should not be judgemental about other souls.

The fact that you picked up this book indicates that you have travelled a substantial distance on this journey. The following test may further help you to locate your co-ordinates with reference to your soul evolution.

The test is about the first five stages, infant to old. Once you are in the transcendental stage you will not feel the need to take this test as you have almost reached your destination.

There are ten questions for each stage. For each question there are two boxes with 'Agree' or 'Disagree' as an option. You can tick the option that appeals you the most. A tick on 'Agree' gives you one point and on 'Disagree' gives you zero. Add up your score in each stage.

So, let's begin...

Infant Soul Test

		Agree	Disagree
1.	My life revolves around my insecurities and fears.	☐	☐
2.	Any change, or unfamiliar situations, places and people make me extremely nervous and anxious.	☐	☐
3.	People often call me gullible and naive.	☐	☐

4.	I often feel confused and overwhelmed in the crowd.	☐	☐
5.	I am deeply interested in learning survival skills, because I am often gripped by mortal fear.	☐	☐
6.	I am highly superstitious by nature.	☐	☐
7.	Safety and security of me and my family is my topmost priority.	☐	☐
8.	I always feel that I am a misfit in the mainstream society.	☐	☐
9.	I consider myself a down-to-earth, simple person with very basic needs.	☐	☐
10.	Things like philosophy, arts, spirituality, fame or wealth do not interest me.	☐	☐

Baby Soul Test

		Agree	**Disagree**
1.	I like to follow the rules set by the society.	☐	☐
2.	I prefer to follow someone, than to lead.	☐	☐
3.	I feel extremely guilty when I go against the set norms.	☐	☐
4.	I consider myself a highly disciplined and meticulous person and I set strict rules for myself.	☐	☐

5.	For me things in life can only fall in one of the two categories: Right or Wrong. It is my prime duty to do what is Right.	☐	☐
6.	I am very religious and follow the rituals or sermons dedicatedly. I believe my religion is the only true religion.	☐	☐
7.	I want to play a significant or meaningful role in an institution, political party or a religious group. Feeling a sense of belonging to a community is important to me.	☐	☐
8.	For me, only my opinions are important.	☐	☐
9.	People often call me orthodox and conservative.	☐	☐
10.	I feel very comfortable in a mundane job. I prefer not being involved in demanding careers.	☐	☐

Young soul test

		Agree	Disagree
1.	I feel irritated and agitated when people don't listen to me.	☐	☐
2.	For me, work comes before anything in life, including relationships.	☐	☐
3.	People often feel I am dominating and bossy.	☐	☐

4. I consider myself highly skilled in whatever I do. ☐ ☐
5. Acquiring degrees and qualifications makes me feel superior. ☐ ☐
6. I can go to any extent to earn money, fame and power. ☐ ☐
7. The fear of losing my social status and material possessions, often gives me sleepless nights. ☐ ☐
8. I love fancy cars, exotic food, and luxurious house with all modern amenities. I like style and brand. ☐ ☐
9. I like to be seen as a successful and self-made person. ☐ ☐
10. I decide my self-worth based on my assets and belongings. ☐ ☐

Mature Soul

	Agree	Disagree
1. I prefer keeping away from confrontation. I choose co-operation over competition.	☐	☐
2. I am most often the first to help or emotionally support a friend or family member.	☐	☐
3. I am sensitive by nature. I often go through emotional turmoil and inner conflict, and suffer from anxiety, guilt and fears.	☐	☐

4. I always try to see other people's perspective in any issue. One of my interests is learning psychology. ☐ ☐
5. I want to live an authentic life. I am conscious about myself and my life. ☐ ☐
6. I am more concerned with inner growth and self discovery. I have been looking for answers to fundamental question such as, "who am I", "What is my purpose", or "what happens after death". ☐ ☐
7. I see myself as more broadminded than conservative. ☐ ☐
8. I have a deep desire to express myself. ☐ ☐
9. For me real personal success is harmonious and lasting relationships. ☐ ☐
10. I am often drawn to artistic, philosophical and humanitarian pursuit. ☐ ☐

Old Soul Test

	Statement	Agree	Disagree
1.	I tend to look at life with a bird's eye perspective, rather than a detail-orientated one.	☐	☐
2.	My biggest qualities are wisdom, compassion and thoughtfulness.	☐	☐

3.	I enjoy reading self-help books more than fashion, politics and finance.	☐	☐
4.	I feel uninterested in gossips, idle talks, degrees, job promotions or discussions on stocks.	☐	☐
5.	I see myself as reflective and insightful. I tend to feel emotions or passions intensely.	☐	☐
6.	I have a strong internal desire to seek ultimate universal truth.	☐	☐
7.	I tend to be a mentor and counselor to people around me. People are more likely to come to me for my advice when they face a challenge.	☐	☐
8.	I feel my interests are much different from people of my age. When I was young, I enjoyed having conversations with people older to me.	☐	☐
9.	I believe in the larger plan of the universe and have strong faith that ultimately everything is happening for our good.	☐	☐
10.	I have a deep feeling that I have lived many lives before the present one. I feel I have an understanding of the fragility and transience of physical life.	☐	☐

Conclusion

Out of the five soul stages, you belong to a stage in which you score the maximum. Sometimes, you may get similar results for two stages. For example, you score 7 points in mature and old soul stage. This may mean that you are at the last levels of mature soul or just stepped in the old soul stage. At any stage, when you go to the next one, you may carry the reminiscences from the previous stage. You can analyse your result with this reference. The results may also vary depending on your state of mind. So avoid being self-critical and don't be too harsh on yourself.

We need to understand that we are always at the right place in the evolution journey, exactly where we are meant to be. Ultimately, we are all moving ahead perfectly on this path and are always divinely guided and protected.

Reflections

Reflections

THE JOURNEY AHEAD

During one of my regression sessions, I had a profound experience during which my life's purpose was revealed to me. It was a session that completely transformed my life. Somehow, I always knew that I was not cut out for a corporate job, but was not sure what I was supposed to do until I received this. However, a clear vision of my life's purpose during the session encouraged me to take a leap of faith, by giving up my corporate career. The journey was not easy. I faced challenges at every step. But with utmost certainty I can say that I have been always guided and protected. Each challenge always took me a step closer to my purpose.

Past life regression has given a definite direction to my life. It has provided answers to the most intriguing questions about life and life after life. It has given me a higher understanding about process of soul evolution and the larger universal plan, thus changing my perspective. I no longer look at life the way I used to 15 years back. I understand the reason for challenges planted in my life and I look at every such incident as an opportunity to grow and evolve. My life has gained a deeper meaning and helped me live each moment with greater awareness. I often ask myself, 'How can I contribute to the process of universal evolution?'

Past life regression has also helped me heal a lot of issues. It has taught me to take responsibility for my actions. It has helped me build deep and long-lasting relationships and has given me an access to the vast ocean of knowledge. It has enriched my life in various ways, by bringing a paradigm shift.

I am sure you must have got answers to most of your questions by now, but please don't stop at that. Strengthen your faith in the fact that you were born with an inherent purpose which will be revealed to you through your intuition, synchronicities and spiritual experiences. Remember that before birth you chose this body and the circumstances and carefully planned the opportunities offered to you. If there are any past memories pulling you back, cut the strings of bondage by practicing forgiveness. Relieve the impactful memories of the past through the process of regression.

Recognize your true power and potential, unearth the hidden talents and explore your dreams. Be the creator of your own destiny.

My prayers and best wishes are always with you...

I AM DIVINE

I am the One, I am Divine,

The Purpose of my Life is, Rise and Shine…

Happiness, Compassion, Peace is Mine,

Filled with Love, and Light Divine

Faith, Trust, Courage and Love,

Forgiveness, Gratitude, All combine

No Stress No Worry, Nor any Problems

My Inner Voice tells me, All is fine

I am not the Body, I am the Soul,

I glow inside, Like a Sun-Shine

I have my Home, Deep within,

Part of Divine, Yours and Mine.

This is my Journey, of many Lifetimes
I choose my Route, to the finishing line
When to let go, & when to Align,
The Universe always, gives me a Sign

Let's all Join, & Walk hand in hand
Towards a New World, that we can Define
The World of our Own, a Special Design
Full of Love & Peace, Joy & Shine.

I AM DIVINE...

Reflections